HE BENT DOWN ~~TO KISS HER~~ MOUTH...

From the first instant she responded with a passionate enjoyment. Her senses seemed to flower and expand. She had never known it was possible to feel as she did now, and still did not realize how much her astonishment told him.

"This has never happened to you before, has it, my treasure?" he asked presently.

"I've been married six months," she reminded him.

"Married perhaps. But never loved."

"And never in love until I met you," she whispered.

ROSALBA

Sheila Bishop

FAWCETT COVENTRY • NEW YORK

PART ONE

AN IRREGULAR ESTABLISHMENT

Rosalba Carlow had been married five months when she caught her husband trying to forge Sir Augustus Rainham's signature.

It was a gray autumn afternoon in 1769, and she had meant to go out and buy some ribbon for trimming a hat. When she reached the front door of their Half Moon Street lodging, she realized that she had forgotten her pattern of green silk; she ran back up the stairs and into their handsome second-floor parlor, to find him hunched over the table with an air of extreme mental and physical concentration. He had not heard her come in.

"What are you doing?" she asked.

He started so violently that a small sheet of paper flew off the table, and she picked it up. It was Gus Rainham's acknowledgment of a gaming loss. *Owed to Mr. Carlow £380. A. Rainham.* The paper on which Carlow had actually been writing was still on the table, the ink shining wet. He put his arm across to stop her seeing it. This was enough to arouse her curiosity. She tweaked it up and stared at the words. They were not in his usual neat hand but in a very good imitation of the young baronet's shaky scrawl. *Owed to Mr. Carlow £820.* And then, over and over again, the carefully copied signature.

"You were planning to rob him—to pretend he'd lost eight hundred pounds. You thought he wouldn't remember, because he was drunk."

Carlow flushed defensively.

"It was only a jest. I wanted to see how much he would recall. He's so rich and so careless, he deserves to be taught a lesson."

Rosalba knew he was lying. He didn't glance away from her, as liars were said to do, he stared straight into her face, his light blue eyes beautiful and empty, as though he was not really there behind them. He was very good-looking in a dandified way, with his fair skin, spruce brown wig, and the expensive clothes that set off his slim figure, but she had come to recognize this pose of innocent frankness for the sham it was. He had gazed at her in just that way when she had caught him kissing the chambermaid at a Newmarket inn, when he had tried to buy a gold snuffbox on credit, when they had left a Cambridge posting house very early in the morning and she was almost sure he had not paid the bill.

She said tartly, "I don't know about teaching people lessons. Isn't it time you yourself learned to keep your hands from picking and stealing?"

"Need you be such a sanctimonious little prude? We've got to live, haven't we? And considering I took you out of that moldering parsonage without a penny piece, the least you can do is to spare me your sermons."

"Very well—no sermons. I'll just remind you that you can be hanged for forgery."

"And much you'd care if I was!" he shouted furiously. "You've made it pretty plain how little you care for me, with your whey face and your body as cold as a fish—I should never have taken up with you, it's been the ruin of my chances!"

There was some real expression in his eyes, a glitter of intense dislike, as he stamped out of the room, almost colliding with the servant who was bringing in the coals.

"'Ad a lover's tiff?" inquired the old woman sympathetically, setting down the heavy steel scuttle and stooping to build up the fire. "Never you mind, my pretty dear. 'E'll soon be back to say 'e's sorry."

"Yes, I expect he will," replied Rosalba.

Because she and Carlow were both young and handsome, old Sarah had got it into her head that they had made an imprudent love match and were now suffering from the pangs of their excessive passion.

And if we were, it would serve us right, thought Rosalba when Sarah had gone. This is the sort of fix girls get into through running away with plausible scoundrels. But I got here from doing what I was told. It was a bitter reflection.

She was nineteen years old and an orphan. Her father, Captain John York, had died when she was ten, after a long and painful illness caused by wounds which he had received in Canada, during the struggle with France, which was now called, in retrospect, the Seven Years War. While he was ill the Yorks had been living in a remote Suffolk village where the rector was his distant cousin. After his death, the Reverend Josiah Chalkey had suggested that Mrs. York had better stay on at White Lodge with Rosalba, her only child. They had lived there in simple comfort and content. Mrs. York had spent what spare money they had on sending Rosalba to a good boarding school in Norwich. She herself had been very well educated, and she wanted her daughter to have the same accomplishments. It had been clear from her infancy that Rosalba was going to be a beauty; that was why they had given her such a fanciful name—she was their White Rose of York. As soon as she left school, she and her mother would go to some watering place like Bath or Tonbridge, and there she would find plenty of suitors—the kind of eligible and dashing young men who did not exist in their corner of Suffolk. Rosalba adored her pretty, romantic mother and believed it all.

How differently their dreams had ended. A month after Rosalba left school, her mother had died of a putrid fever, caught from a tracing peddler who had come into the house to display his linens and laces.

Rosalba was so stunned with grief that it took her some time to realize the awkwardness of her position. What was to be done with her? She certainly could not stay on at White Lodge alone, a girl of seventeen. She had no surviving uncles or aunts on her father's side, and her mother had never spoken of any relations at all (a rather odd circumstance which had never puzzled Rosalba, who had accepted her parents just as they were).

She had been taken into the rectory as a temporary measure, and after a few weeks Mr. and Mrs. Chalkey felt obliged to offer her a home, which she had felt obliged to accept. They were a thrifty joyless couple with two unmarried daughters a little older than Rosalba, and they did not want another girl on their hands. Once she overheard them talking about her.

"How are Hetty and Maria to find husbands, I should like to know, with that saucy little butterfly forever putting herself forward?" This was Mrs. Chalkey.

"I think you are unjust, my dear," replied the parson.

"Rosalba does not mean to be pert. It is all the fault of that new-fangled school her mother sent her to. What a fool the poor woman was, wasting her money so. At least we can congratulate ourselves that our girls will be better provided for. No sensible man chooses a penniless wife."

"Of course no one is going to *marry* Rosalba York! That is half the trouble, for as long as she is about, the men are not going to think of marrying anyone else."

This made Rosalba feel very uncomfortable, and the next two years were cheerless indeed. She did not dislike Hetty and Maria, who never resented her as their mother did, but the interests of the whole family were very limited and she saw no hope of escaping from a life of restriction and loneliness—until Mr. Edgar Carlow appeared on the scene.

He was staying at the manor as a guest of the squire, whose sister, Miss Elizabeth Proudfoot, had apparently met him in London. Miss Elizabeth was thirty-five, and this seemed so ancient to the girls at the parsonage that they never suspected her of hoping to marry an Adonis of twenty-six. Having missed this point, they naturally failed to realize that the squire had taken a hard look at the visitor and told his sister she was making a fool of herself. It was a complete surprise when Mr. Carlow started calling at the parsonage and paying a great deal of attention to Rosalba.

She was flattered and excited, and when he actually asked her to marry him she was so grateful she almost accepted him on the spot. She had enough good sense to return a cautious answer and ask for time to think. What should she do? She did not love him, she was not even sure that she liked him very much—after all, she hardly knew him—but few girls had the luck to fall in love with their bridegrooms before marriage, and it should not be difficult to grow fond of such an attractive man. And what other suitors could she expect? Some rough farmer perhaps, ignorant and boorish, or an old widower who wanted an unpaid housekeeper. She would be far wiser to marry Mr. Carlow; the Chalkeys certainly thought so, and made it plain that it was her duty to dispose of herself so conveniently. Mr. Chalkey had talked to the young man and discovered that he belonged to a good West Country family and would come into possession of a moderate fortune on his marriage. He had been told that Rosalba had nothing of her own and said it made no difference. This, more than anything, settled the question, for she was touched by the idea of his loving her in such a disinterested way and felt they ought to be happy together.

They were married as quickly as possible and set out for London. Their wedding night was an anticlimax, for Carlow drank rather a lot at supper and seized on her with an urgency she could neither understand nor share. He then fell asleep and snored. Rosalba was not exactly disappointed—she had heard that women did not always enjoy this aspect of marriage—but she was puzzled. Was it to perform these hasty, undignified actions that some people deserted their homes, ruined their hopes and made themselves miserable for ever after? The whole thing seemed very odd, but perhaps she would get used to it.

When they arrived in London and called on Carlow's lawyer in Lincoln's Inn, there was a much worse shock in store, for it turned out that his grandmother's bequest, which he was to inherit on his marriage, was much smaller than he had expected. The property in Gloucestershire was already encumbered, and if he sold it straightaway, he would not get a quarter of the price he was hoping for.

"I believe it was your grandmother's wish that you should settle at Wickley," said Mr. Meade. "If you nursed the estate carefully, you would soon be free from debt."

He was quite a young man, his face thin and sensitive between the heavy tresses of his lawyer's long wig.

"Settle in that damned hole!" exclaimed Carlow. "You must be mad. And I reckon I've been swindled. I didn't go to all the trouble of getting married just to inherit a few beggarly hundreds and a broken-down pigsty!"

Rosalba could still feel the sickening shock of pain and bewilderment as his words had hit her like a physical blow. Mr. Meade had been horribly embarrassed. It was his glance of compassion that had forced her to pull herself together.

Sitting up very straight, she said to her husband, "I must commiserate with you, sir. I don't know which of us is most to be pitied."

This checked Carlow, who said hurriedly that she mustn't

take him up so; naturally he hadn't meant that he was sorry he'd married her.

But of course he had meant exactly that, thought Rosalba, staring into the fire. By now she had unraveled the whole story. He was a black sheep who had been cast out by his family after a long succession of disgraceful episodes, which he was apt to brag about when he was drunk; only his old grandmother had gone on believing that he might reform. She had left him a house and a little money which he was to receive on his marriage, when presumably he would have turned over a new leaf. The poor old woman could not have imagined that he would marry simply to get hold of the estate, and to start with he had not meant to do so. He had made several attempts to marry an heiress. But all these ladies had watchful relations who saw what he was after, and in the end he was so desperate to get hold of the legacy that he was prepared to marry a penniless orphan because her guardians were so anxious to be rid of her that they would not make too many inquiries about him.

Once she began to realize this, Rosalba found that she could no longer conjure up any pretense of affection for her husband. She could tolerate him and try to make allowances. That was all.

It was summer, not the time to be in town. They set off on a tour of the various places where race meetings were held. They had gone to Ascot, Epsom, Newmarket and as far afield as Chester, anywhere that Carlow could follow the horses by day and play cards at night with a selected party of acquaintances.

In spite of everything, Rosalba was not actively unhappy. She enjoyed the races, the beautiful galloping horses and the lively crowds. If Carlow was winning they would sometimes go to a theater or a race ball. It was all new to her, and very much more amusing than life with the Chalkeys. The card parties she found tedious. The guests were all men and she was not expected to play, but Carlow liked her to be there, to pour out the wine and make herself agreeable for the first hour or so. Now she wondered whether the presence of his young wife had lent an air of domestic respectability to those little gatherings, and whether this had made it easier for him

11

to take money off his victims, by fair means or foul. For there was no doubt, now she faced the fact, that he was a professional gambler who lived by playing with men less experienced than himself. She was not sure if he actually cheated at cards. It would hardly be necessary, if he was prepared to fuddle his guests with drink and forge their handwriting.

Though she hoped this last effort might be unusual, for he had been short of funds since their return to London. The men here were less gullible than in the provinces, and if they wanted to play high they went to clubs or gaming halls.

Rosalba was still sitting in her hat and cloak; she got up and went into the adjoining bedroom to take them off. Standing in front of the glass to arrange her cap, she studied her appearance dispassionately. She was slender and fairly tall, with an oval face narrowing into a determined chin. Her name had been well chosen, for she had very white skin with an almost opaque velvet texture. She had brilliant dark eyes and dark hair, piled up on her head in the modern fashion and gleaming under the lace lappets. She had a well-shaped mouth, the lips so naturally smooth and warm, a rose color, that people often thought she painted them. Carlow had called her whey-faced, she thought, and as cold as a fish. But then he really liked florid boisterous barmaids. She had found this out too late.

She was not sure when he would come back or what sort of a mood he would be in, so it was a relief when he appeared in good time for dinner and bringing a friend.

"I told Dan he could take pot luck with us," he announced in a loud careless voice which implied that he had graciously pardoned Rosalba for the sin of criticizing him.

"Good evening, Mr. Robinson," said Rosalba. "Did you warn them to lay an extra place, my dear? Then we may as well go down."

The Carlows rented the second floor of the house, comprising a drawing room and bedroom, and also the use of a dining room on the ground floor to eat their dinner in; they took this meal at half past four, a later and more fashionable hour than the family of their landlord, Mr. Stone, a clerk in the Treasury.

"Well now, this is very snug," said Dan Robinson, as he

12

examined the fleet of tureens and sauce boats on the starched white cloth, and accepted helpings of mutton, kidneys, rice, and several vegetables.

He was a sharp-looking man, passing for a gentleman, with a touch of vulgarity about him, and Rosalba thought him quite as great a rogue as her husband, though somehow his very flashiness made him seem less of a fraud. Anyone who was deceived by Dan Robinson was asking to be taken in. He and Carlow returned to a conversation they had been having when they arrived.

"So Gus Rainham turned up after all? I think he was in two minds about coming. He's a stupid, timid fellow."

"Are you acquainted with Sir Augustus?" asked Rosalba, faintly surprised.

"Bless you, ma'am, I've known all the Rainhams since I was in my cradle. My father was the old man's agent and land steward up at Ashwin, and my brother succeeded him there. Not that young Gus ever goes near the place these days. He's far too busy spending his uncle's money before his family can stop him."

"What do you mean by that?" inquired Carlow. "Surely he has control of his capital? I know he came into the devil of a lot from that younger brother of his father's, the one who went out to India and became a nabob. I took it for granted when you introduced me to him..."

Carlow saw Rosalba watching him and left the rest of the sentence unfinished. So that was it, she thought. Robinson had brought them together because he knew the silly young man was a fat pigeon for Carlow to pluck.

"Oh yes, it's all his," Dan Robinson was saying. "Apart from Ashwin itself, which is entailed. He has the full disposal of everything else, but the trouble is, you see, that he's such a feeble fellow. He's the seventh baronet, head of an ancient line and all the rest, but he's the fool of the family and they let him know it. He's afraid of his uncle and aunt, he's even a little afraid of his wife, Lady Alicia, or at least of her noble relatives, and worst of all he's scared stiff of his cousin Hugh—an arrogant, domineering brute Hugh Rainham is; he can't stand the sight of me, and it's mutual, I can tell you!"

Carlow laughed and poured him another glass of claret.

13

"Can it be that he thinks you are a bad influence on his weak-minded cousin?"

"That's about it. And that's why I wondered whether Gus would have the temerity to come and play cards with any friend of mine."

Gus would have done better to stay away, thought Rosalba. She had met him for the first time yesterday evening: a pallid young man with one of those loose, wet mouths, and a conceited manner which probably covered a constant fear of not measuring up to his proper stature in the world. Not a very reliable person, and one could not blame his family for trying to keep him in order. All the same, she was a little sorry for him.

The men began to speak of something else.

It was several days later that Carlow asked Rosalba, "Would you like to go to that new exhibition of paintings everyone is talking about? I suppose it must be worth seeing."

"Oh yes, do let us go," she said, delighted to have the chance, for it was not the sort of entertainment he often took her to.

She dressed with care in her new dove-colored poplin; she did not put on a hoop, for she knew the rooms would be crowded, and the quilted petticoat gave her skirt quite enough shape and buoyancy. Her short black polonaise cloak had pale blue trimmings that matched the curled feathers in her small hat, and she felt as elegant as any of the fine people who were paying their half-crowns and streaming up the stairs in the house just off Bond Street where the exhibition was being held.

The gallery was certainly full of ladies and gentlemen; the pictures hung thick on the walls, right up to the ceiling. They were mostly history paintings of classical subjects. Rosalba found herself staring at one which was supposed to represent Queen Zenobia at the siege of Palmyra. She was trying to make out what was going on (not easy, for the figures seemed a long way off in a landscape of brooding austerity) when Carlow said, "Why, there are the Rainhams. What a happy coincidence. If we move in their direction, I daresay he will present us to his wife. You would like that."

She turned reluctantly. She knew that his surprise was

14

simulated, not merely because she knew the false notes in his voice by now; she also understood at once why he had wasted five shillings to come and look at pictures which did not interest him. He must have heard somehow that the Rainhams meant to visit the exhibition this morning. Dan Robinson had made it plain that the young man was nervous of associating with dubious characters whom his family disapproved of. Carlow probably thought that if he could engineer a meeting between their two wives, she might ingratiate herself with Lady Alicia.

She was unwilling to do this. She did not at all wish to play the innocent, ladylike sheep who was to spread her mantle of respectability over the wolf. She hoped that Gus Rainham might not see them. He was standing next to a rather insipid young woman with no eyebrows, who was dutifully listening to a dark, decisive man, apparently an authority on the pictures—he might almost have stepped out of one of them, for he had a distinctly Roman nose.

Sir Gus was gazing vacantly around him; he caught sight of the Carlows, and immediately came over.

"Didn't think to see you here," he said to Carlow. "Don't tell me you enjoy this sort of stuff?"

"My wife does."

"So does mine," said Gus Rainham gloomily. Then he smirked at Rosalba with a fatuous gallantry and said, "I expect you like all pretty things, ma'am—so pretty as you are yourself. I've got a house full of treasures—better than any of this rubbish—like to show them to you some time."

"How very kind of you, Sir Augustus," said Rosalba politely.

Having heard that his house was somewhere in the Midlands, and that he never went near it, she felt this was a harmless response.

He then disconcerted her by saying that Liston was only an hour's ride away in Surrey. It was the house his uncle had built on his return from India.

"I have heard it described as a palace," said Carlow. "We should very much like to see it, shouldn't we, my love?"

At this moment the dark man advanced purposefully on

Gus and said, "Alicia is becoming a little tired. I think we should leave."

"Oh, very well. But first let me present you to Mrs. Carlow. My cousin Mr. Hugh Rainham, ma'am."

Mr. Rainham looked down his Roman nose at Rosalba and made her the very slightest pretense of a bow. He ignored her husband altogether. He was impatient to get his cousin away, taking him firmly by the elbow and steering him through the press of people.

As they moved off, Rosalba heard him say quite audibly, "My dear Gus, why do you always gravitate toward these third-rate adventurers? Can't you see that they simply want to take money off you?"

2

One afternoon in the following week Carlow said: "I'm expecting Gus Rainham to come round this evening for a hand of picquet. I want you to make yourself especially pleasant to him."

"I hope I should never be disagreeable to a guest."

"No, I don't suppose you would. But this is important, Rosalba. I need money badly. I thought I could borrow some from the little monster—only it seems he isn't so lavish and open-handed as one might imagine, unless he gets something he wants in return. And what he wants at the moment, according to Dan Robinson, even more than a run of luck at the tables, is a little encouragement from you. Dan says you have quite captured his fancy. Diverting, isn't it?"

"Very," said Rosalba with distaste, thinking of Sir Augustus, white and flabby, and his greedy, babyish mouth. "You think that if I smile at him sweetly enough, he'll come across with a loan?"

"Well, not precisely. We'll handle it a little differently." Carlow got up and began to walk about the room. "I'll go out—leave you alone together while I fetch another bottle of wine; that will give him his opportunity, and if you manage things properly—"

"Good God, are you suggesting I should let him seduce me? I knew you were a liar and thief, Carlow. I did not realise you were the kind of man who plays pander for his own wife!"

"You are quite mistaken—of course I don't intend you to become his mistress. In fact, if I ever suspected you of infidelity, I'd give you a sound thrashing," announced Carlow pompously, as though such a highly moral proceeding would prove him a model husband. "All you have to do this evening is to lead Rainham on a little, and then cry out at the first sign of familiarity. I shall come straight back into the room. You can then tell me that he has made an assault on your virtue, and after that I doubt we'll have any trouble with him. His wife is expecting a child, and he will be terrified of a scandal."

"I see," said Rosalba, her voice dry with anger. "You want me to lay a trap, so that we can make him pay for what he didn't get. I think I'd prefer to set up as an honest harlot and give good value for money."

"Don't you talk to me like that, you scolding shrew," he threw back at her. "You've been nothing but an expense and a burden these last five months. It's high time you earned your keep, instead of sneering at everything I do with that sharp tongue of yours. Rather set up as a harlot, would you? Well, I daresay. It's in your blood."

"What do you mean?" she demanded, completely at a loss.

"I suppose you never knew that your mother was the misbegotten brat of some little seamstress or milliner who came to grief in the usual manner. The father provided for the child and saw to it that she found a husband who wasn't too particular. Old Chalkey felt obliged to tell me so at our famous interview. He pieced together the story from your mother's papers after she died, and he was so shocked he hadn't even told his wife. He saw it as a blot on his own family escutcheon! But he felt it his duty to warn me in case you had inherited any dangerous tendencies. We were very solemn about it," said Carlow, laughing at the recollection and adding unkindly, "Perhaps the memory of your grandmama will teach you to be a little less ladylike and high-minded."

"You've made it all up—I don't believe a word of it!" exclaimed Rosalba.

But she did believe it, all the same. She threw herself onto the sofa and burst into tears.

She was not weeping over the sins of her unknown grandmother, nor for the shadow they cast on her own ancestry; she was thinking of her mother, realizing for the first time how forlorn and friendless most of her life must have been, apart from the few happy years of her marriage. And she had tried so hard to keep her pathetic secret, only to have it dug up by moralizing Cousin Chalkey after she was dead and made a topic for Carlow's flippant scorn. Rosalba did not often cry. She considered that tears—like the vapors—indicated a feeble character, and all through the shocks and setbacks of her life with Carlow she had bitten back her emotions and assumed a brave composure. Now she had let herself break down she found it hard to stop. She buried her face in the cushions, and when Carlow tried to come near her, she screamed at him to go away.

"Dinner's on the table."

"I don't care. I don't want any dinner."

He left her, and presently Sarah came in, bringing her a bowl of broth and many commiserations.

"There now, ma'am. What's he been doing to you?"

Rosalba wanted to say, "He told me my grandmother was a strumpet"; it sounded so very ridiculous that she almost laughed. She dried her eyes, accepting the broth, which made her feel a good deal better. She was still sitting by the fire when Carlow came upstairs again. She decided to ignore him.

He gave her a sideways glance but said nothing and began making his preparations for the evening, moving between the two rooms, setting out the card table.

Rosalba stood up, saying with a firmness she did not feel well, "I shall spend the evening in the other room. I don't wish to meet your friend, so please don't disturb me."

"Very well," he said in a voice that was almost placating. "Just as you wish."

It had been much easier than she had expected. She took a lighted candle and walked into the bedroom, half intending to lock the door, but the key was not there, and anyway it seemed quite unnecessary, for her violent outburst had apparently had a very good effect. Perhaps she ought to make

18

such scenes more often? She put the candle on the bedside table and sat down on the only chair.

She heard Gus Rainham arrive, and heard the two men talking but not what they were saying, for the door was thick and solid, and the table where they soon settled to play was at the far end of the drawing room. Rosalba yawned. She felt cold and dejected and the chair was not at all comfortable; the bed looked much more inviting, only she could not lie down in her stays.

She decided to undress, and when she had done so she slipped under the quilt, wearing only her shift. Lulled by the warmth and ease, she drifted into a consoling sleep.

She was waked some time later by loud sounds from the next room: a falling chair and breaking glass. She jerked up in a daze, not knowing what time it was nor why the single candle was still burning. The door opened and two figures appeared in the rectangle of light. Carlow propelling Gus Rainham, who sagged helplessly as he stumbled forward.

"Sir Augustus has been overcome by the heat of the fire.... Hold up, my dear fellow.... He should lie down for a while."

"Well, he can't lie down in here," exclaimed Rosalba, pulling the quilt up to her chin. "I'm in bed. Let him lie on the drawing-room carpet if he must. I suppose the horrid creature is drunk again."

Carlow paid no attention. He brought his sottish guest right into the room and left him swaying at the foot of the bed. Then he himself went out, closing the door.

"Carlow!" cried Rosalba indignantly. "What are you thinking of? Come back at once!"

She still imagined he was merely being thoughtless and inept, until she heard the astonishing sound of a key turning in the lock. Carlow had deliberately shut them in. He had never relinquished his original plan, and he was going to carry it out, with or without her cooperation. She heard his footsteps retreating towards the landing. Presumably he was going to fetch some witnesses. And a very pretty tableau he would have to show them.

She said sharply to Gus Rainham, "You had better pull yourself together and use your wits—if you have any."

19

It was obvious that he could hardly stand, but he reached out a faltering hand in her direction, and his sweating, sickly features took on an ingratiating leer.

"Charming siren—ready to play naughty games?"

He made an ambitious lurch and nearly fell down.

"Oh, for pity's sake!" said Rosalba, exasperated.

She must get out of bed, and could only hope he was too far gone to be further inflamed by the vision of a female in her shift. Hugging the quilt round her like a cloak, she scrambled across the room to reach a chintz wrapper, which she put on to make herself more presentable. Then she began to hammer on the panels of the door, demanding to be let out.

Behind her Gus had collapsed on to the bed.

"Get up," said Rosalba, looking around. "You will make everything worse."

She hurried to the washstand, dipped a towel into the water jug and handed it to her supposed seducer, telling him to bathe his head and face. His eyes were horribly out of focus. She wondered if he was not drunk after all, but drugged. Probably Carlow had put something in his wine.

She ran back to the door and caught the sound of several people approaching. Voices. The precise accent of their landlord, Mr. Stone, the Treasury clerk.

"...if you say so, Mr. Carlow. I should not have thought it possible.... If the man has such a bad character, why did you leave him alone with your wife?"

"Let me out of here!" shouted Rosalba, rattling the door handle.

"My dear, you will be perfectly safe now," said Carlow in a theatrical manner. "Has that villain harmed you? He shall pay dearly for this!"

"Don't be so stupid. Of course he hasn't harmed me. And I'm not going to let you make money out of him," Rosalba added.

"I daresay Mrs. Carlow received the gentleman quite willingly, sir." This was prim and disapproving Mrs. Stone. "We are not used to such scandalous carryings-on in our house, and what's more I won't stand for it."

At this point a new voice was heard, resonant and faintly familiar.

20

"I am looking for Sir Augustus Rainham. The servant said I should find him here."

There was an immediate clamor from both the Stones informing him that Sir Augustus had locked himself into the bedroom with Mrs. Carlow, and what a shocking thing it was to happen in a respectable house.

"Shocking indeed," said the deep voice derisively. "Gus, are you in there?"

Gus was sitting up now, frightened and shaky.

"It's my cousin Hugh," he whispered to Rosalba.

She remembered now—the Roman senator at the exhibition of paintings.

"Gus! Open the door."

"I can't, Hugh. It—it seems to be locked. I haven't got the key."

"Find it then. It must be somewhere in the room. The woman's hidden it."

"I have not hidden it!" Rosalba called back. "The door was locked from the outside, and if you want the key, you will have to take it off my husband."

Predictably, Carlow began to abuse her, saying that she was a wicked wanton, she had betrayed him with her rich lover and he had caught them in the act. He didn't get any further, for there was a scuffle—it sounded as though Mr. Rainham had picked him up and shaken him—and then there was a cry of triumph. The key had been found.

A moment later the door was flung open and Rosalba almost stepped into the arms of Hugh Rainham as he came into the room. They both stopped. His eyes were a cool hazel. His comprehensive glance ran over the shape of her body under the thin wrapper; the Stones followed him in, each carrying a branched candlestick, so that the bedroom was suddenly flooded with light and she felt painfully exposed.

Then he stepped past her and addressed his cousin.

"What a fool you are, Gus. Can't I take my eyes off you for five minutes without your falling into the hands of pimps and harpies? Are you never going to learn sense?"

"Nobody asked you to interfere," muttered the baronet, who was now fully conscious but cowed and resentful. He added, "I don't know what brought you here."

"You were due at the Hertfords' ball an hour ago. When you and Alicia failed to arrive, I went round to Grosvenor Street. I found her in tears. She guessed where you had gone. I said I'd fetch you home, so we had best be on our way. And do put your wig straight."

Hugh Rainham seemed able to ignore the lesser persons in the room. Rosalba had withdrawn into the darkest corner and was biting her lip in the anger and humiliation of being called a harpy. The Stones were telling Carlow hc could leave their house tomorrow and take his wife with him (if she was his wife, which they doubted). When they saw the Rainhams departing, however, they scurried after them, anxious to make it plain to these wealthy and well-connected gentlemen that this was a respectable household and nothing so unseemly had ever happened here before.

The Carlows were alone.

He turned on her a glance of such vicious fury that she caught her breath, shrinking even further into the corner. He seized her arm and dragged her into the drawing room, hitting and cuffing her with the flat side of his hand.

"You disloyal bitch! Thought you could get the better of me, did you? I'll make you sorry!"

He gave her a violent push so that she fell heavily to the ground, and then he began to hit and kick her at the same time.

"Stop that!"

Rosalba heard the sharp words through the rain of blows. Then the blows ceased and Carlow turned on the intruder.

"This is my lodging. You've no right of entry here now you've retrieved your precious cousin. How I choose to punish my wife for her misconduct is no concern of yours."

Hugh Rainham paid no attention to this dignified speech. He came to look down at Rosalba, saying: "Are you much hurt? Do you think you can get up?"

"Of course I can."

She was already pulling herself to her feet with the help of a chair. She was badly bruised and trembling so much that she could hardly stand, but she wanted neither help nor pity from this detestable person who had looked at her as though she was naked and then called her a harpy.

Mr. Rainham turned to their landlord, who was still dancing attendance on him.

"Have you a vacant room in the house? I don't think this young woman should be left to the mercy of her protector."

The inflection on the last word was sardonic.

"I'm turning them out of here in the morning, sir," said Stone grimly. "And I daresay he'll give her no more than she deserves."

"That may be. However, she has saved my family from some embarrassment by refusing to back up her accomplice—for whatever reason. So I can afford to feel charitable. And I don't suppose you want a murder on your hands, do you?"

Carlow was standing with his feet apart, and examining his clenched knuckles as though merely waiting for this interlude to end.

Stone, visibly horrified, said something about a room on the attic floor.

"A wise precaution," remarked Mr. Rainham. He stared about at the disordered room. "I came back to collect my cousin's hat. And there it is on the side table. No, don't trouble to see me out. I expect you or your wife will be wanting to take the young woman to her new quarters."

3

Rosalba spent the rest of the night in a cheerless room on the top floor. Carlow had made no objection to this plan—he must know that he would have her to himself soon enough, with all the traditional rights of a husband to bully and persecute her. Rosalba lay on the bare mattress of the unmade bed with only one thin blanket to cover her, shivering and nursing her bruises. She was at once too disturbed and too exhausted either to think clearly or to sleep. She simply endured.

By early morning she was so cold that her chief longing was to get back to her own room so that she could put on some warm clothes, even if it meant braving Carlow. Though it might be wise to wait until there were other people stirring before she did this.

She was listening to various creaks and scrapes and sounds of sweeping, plucking up her courage to face a most unpleasant day, when Mrs. Stone came in without knocking.

"So your fancy man's gone in the night!"

"Gone?" repeated Rosalba. "Gone where?"

"To his own damnation, I suppose. That's where such conduct leads in the end. He must have slipped out in the small hours while we were all asleep. He's taken his clothes and everything he possessed."

"Oh, thank God!" said Rosalba, who immediately felt the most intense relief. She hoped Carlow would go as far away as possible and that she would never have to see him again.

"Well, that's a shocking sentiment for a so-called wife. I suppose you was never married—you may as well confess it now, you bad, shameless wretch."

"Of course we were married."

Rosalba tried to speak with dignity, getting up from the bed and clutching the crumpled chintz wrapper round her. She had noticed that since the admittedly disgraceful scene in her bedroom last night, everyone had begun to assume that she was simply Carlow's mistress. Which seemed unreasonable, for it was only her sense of duty that had kept her with him so long, half aware of his devious ways without being corrupted by them. If I'd been his mistress, she thought, I'd have left him weeks ago.

"You had a proper church wedding?" persisted Mrs. Stone. "Not one of these fudged-up contracts that were put a stop to by law?"

"We were married at Solford Parish Church in Suffolk by the rector, who was my father's cousin."

"Then we can hold you responsible for what Mr. Carlow owes us!" exclaimed the landlady in triumph.

Rosalba hardly took in this threat. She was on her way downstairs. She was brought up short by her first sight of the drawing room. Every drawer had been tipped out onto the carpet, every small ornament removed. In the bedroom the confusion was much worse. Carlow had taken everything portable that was of the slightest value. He had not merely collected his own clothes, he had systematically stripped hers of anything he could sell: embroidered stomachers, lace ruffles, shoe buckles had gone, and so had all her trinkets, including a set of cameos and a crystal necklace left her by her mother. The loss of these made her start to cry, as she had cried yesterday when she thought of her mother's friendless condition. But this would not do, she must not break down. She dressed quickly in a plain gown which had never had any decoration on it for Carlow to tear and spoil. When she went back into the drawing room she found a tray with a very meager breakfast on it.

She was crumbling a dry roll without much appetite when Mr. and Mrs. Stone came in to demand an instant settlement of their account.

"There's a month's rent owing, besides the price of candles and tea that I let you have," the landlady announced, "and a great quantity of wine and brandy Mr. Stone ordered in for your husband, all of which has been drunk. And I must make it plain, ma'am, that you don't leave this house until everything has been paid for."

"But I haven't any money," protested Rosalba, who had just discovered seven shillings in her purse. She was surprised Carlow had not taken that.

"Then you must get hold of some, if you don't want to land in the sponging house."

Rosalba began to feel frightened. The debt was not such a very large one, but it might have been ten thousand pounds for all the hope she had of paying it. Whom could she turn to? There was absolutely no one. She thought despairingly of the Chalkeys—would they help her out of this fix? Even if they could afford to, which she doubted. After all, they had encouraged her to marry the handsome stranger from London; they could not have guessed what he was really like. Or had they? It struck her for the first time that when she left Suffolk the Chalkeys had made a decent show of wishing her well but without expressing any hope of future meetings. She had scarcely noticed this on her wedding day (being secretly delighted to part with them) but it now seemed very odd. If they had believed that she was going to be securely established in good society, the elder Chalkeys would have considered it her duty to invite her cousins Maria and Hetty for long visits and try to find husbands for them. And they would have told her so. Probably they had guessed all along that there was something wrong with Carlow; not his criminal tendencies perhaps, but they might have gathered that he was a spendthrift and a gamester. And people who would hand over an inexperienced girl to such a husband were likely to turn a deaf ear when inevitably she needed to be rescued.

Was there anyone else? Thinking back over the uneasy months of her marriage, Rosalba remembered Mr. Meade, the lawyer who had dealt with Carlow's inheritance, and who had been so obviously disgusted by the way he spoke of his marriage. Mr. Meade was quite young and very agreeable. He was used to acting for the Carlow family, so perhaps he could settle these debts.

Rosalba wrote him a note, and the Stones allowed their pantry boy to take it to Lincoln's Inn. While he was gone, Rosalba began to sort and pack her belongings.

A reply was brought back within the hour. Mr. Meade was out of town at present but the writer, one Lemuel Briggs, had received instructions that the Carlow family would in no circumstances pay any more of Mr. Edgar Carlow's debts.

So that was that.

"There is no one else I can apply to," Rosalba told the Stones.

"Then you'll have to go to prison, my fine lady, until you can pay every penny you owe us. That'll teach you to defraud honest people," said Mrs. Stone with a cruel satisfaction.

"I am very sorry that my husband has cheated you, but surely you can see that I am as much a victim as you are. He has left me here with nothing, and shutting me up in a debtors' prison will do nothing to settle your account."

Mr. Stone saw the sense of this and was inclined to give way, but his wife was adamant.

"Never fear, she'll find means to pay once she has sampled the alternative."

Rosalba could not imagine why Mrs. Stone thought this. Did she assume that such a young woman must have wealthy friends if she could be made to swallow her pride and appeal to them? Or there was a more sinister idea. Not everyone in a debtors' prison was literally destitute—plenty of the prisoners could afford small luxuries—and if Rosalba was sufficiently desperate she might be induced to earn some money by trading in the one thing she had to sell.

She was by now really frightened. Left alone once more, she sat staring into the empty grate and wondering what was to become of her. She heard a man's voice on the landing and a firm step. Could this be the bailiff, or whatever he was called, arriving already to arrest her for debt?

"Good morning, Mrs. Carlow."

The man standing in the doorway was Hugh Rainham.

He looked impressively large, dark and privileged. He wore a coat of dark blue broadcloth with a touch of white at his throat; there was nothing dandified about him unless it was the hint of austerity which, on such an expensively dressed man, must be an affectation.

Rosalba stood up, uncertainly. "If you are looking for my husband, he is not here. He has left me. I should think the Stones might have told you."

"Yes, they did. I hope you will not be offended if I say that you are well rid of him."

"No, why should I be, Mr. Rainham?" she said swiftly. "It is not nearly so offensive as hearing myself called a harpy."

She had thought him insufferably arrogant, not susceptible to criticism from his inferiors, so she was surprised when he flushed, seeming really uncomfortable.

"I'm sorry about that. Which is one of the reasons I came to call on you this morning. To apologize."

"Oh?"

He had advanced into the room; now he laid down his hat and gloves on the table and drew out a chair.

"May I?"

They both sat down.

"I'm afraid I mistook the situation last night," he said. "I was surprised into a whole series of wrong conclusions. Quite unforgivable—though I hope you will forgive me all the same. It was only when I had time to reflect, and when I was able to get something coherent out of my extremely foolish cousin, that I realized how unjust I had been to you. I really am very sorry."

27

This was not quite good enough, thought Rosalba. She had temporarily forgotten the plight she was in, and could think of nothing but Mr. Hugh Rainham and his graceful penitence; she was not going to be blandished so easily.

"I don't know why you should have misjudged me," she remarked. "Directly you arrived on the scene I called out to you through the door that it was my husband who had locked us in. You must have seen at once that I was not a party to his scheme for getting money out of Sir Augustus."

"Yes," he admitted rather hesitantly. "I did realize that. It was clear that you were not prepared to use trickery and extortion. But I'm afraid I was cynical enough to suppose that you might have other designs on my cousin."

"You thought I'd let myself be pawed about by that nasty little toad!" said Rosalba, enraged.

She then realized the indelicacy of what she had said. How could she have been so vulgar? It must be the effect of associating with Carlow and his dreadful friends.

Hugh Rainham said quietly, "I conceived the idea before I had time to observe you properly. And I am sorry Gus is incapable of recognizing a lady when he meets one."

Rosalba found herself blushing. She did not feel she had behaved like a lady, and if Mr. Rainham took her for one, it was more to his credit than hers. If Sir Gus was unprepossessing, his cousin was the absolute reverse. She had never seen a man so magnetically attractive. I should not mind being locked in a bedroom with him, she thought, and was horrified by this new example of her own baser instincts. What could be the matter with her? She glanced away, afraid that he might read her thoughts.

After a pause, he asked: "Mrs. Carlow, how did you come to marry such a scoundrel? What were your parents thinking of?"

"My parents are both dead. When I met Mr. Carlow I was living in a Suffolk village with distant relatives who were perhaps as easily deceived as I was about his true character."

She gave him a brief outline of her past history, without letting it appear how anxious the Chalkeys had been to get rid of her. She sensed that she was an object of pity to this man, and the idea of playing on his compassion disgusted her. She could not bear to humiliate herself any further. She made the Chalkeys sound like benevolent but unworldly people who thought they had helped her to make a good marriage.

"I expect you will return to them now?" he suggested.

"I daresay I shall." She was cautiously evasive. "I have some commitments to attend to first."

"If you mean paying your husband's debts to Mr. and Mrs. Stone, that has been attended to."

She stared at him. "What do you mean?"

"I was told the whole story directly I entered the house, and we soon came to a satisfactory arrangement. There is no longer any question of your being arrested for debt."

"But this is nonsensical! Why should you concern yourself with my difficulties? It is very charitable of you, Mr. Rainham, and I'm sure I ought to be most grateful to you, but you must see that I cannot accept favors from—from a gentleman who is not related to me and whom I hardly know."

"I am not putting you under any sort of obligation, I assure you."

"Of course you are—paying all the money we owe! I can't possibly allow it."

"You can't possibly prevent it," he said, smiling slightly. "It is the Stones who had to make a decision. However vindictive they may have been towards you, it is true that they were owed money for services provided, and if they, your creditors, are prepared to accept payment from a third person, I don't think you have any power to interfere. Even though you would prefer to languish in a sponging house rather than let that disagreeable woman receive a penny."

"You know that isn't the reason," she protested. "Of course they need the money. They are not rich, and it is shameful that we should be in debt to them. And there is nothing wrong in gentlemen borrowing from each other. Only I am so awkwardly placed and I don't know what I should do."

"Yes, I understand. You think I am going to ask for something in return. Well, I am."

Rosalba's heart began to beat very fast. She wondered if she was going to receive a dishonorable proposal. She was unable to speak.

29

Hugh Rainham said, "I am going to ask you to overcome your natural scruples and accept a small loan that will enable you to rejoin your friends. There can be no impropriety in your doing this. After all, you must leave this house, and a beautiful young woman cannot wander about London penniless and unprotected. I hope you will allow me to help you meet the expenses of your journey."

"It is very kind of you, sir," murmured Rosalba, ashamed of her suspicions.

She could hardly go on questioning the ulterior motives of a man who was offering her money to return to Suffolk. Her mind was racing. Of course she had no intention of going back to the Chalkeys (perhaps it was lucky she had misled Mr. Rainham about that). Instead she would have to find some sort of employment so that she could keep herself, and what she needed now was a small sum to tide her over while she was finding her feet. She did not think it would be dishonest to pretend she was leaving London and then use his loan to pay for a cheap lodging in some other part of town.

He was relieved that she was ready to take up his offer without arguing, and at once produced a shower of gold coins which he built up into a small pillar and tried to push across the table to her in a nonchalant manner as though they were playing some kind of game.

"That is far too much," she said.

"You will need to travel comfortably inside the coach, and to spend a night or two on the way. And that reminds me, I don't know how often the coaches go to Ipswich, but you will have to spend tonight in London and perhaps tomorrow as well. I suppose you won't care to remain in this house after the way that woman has treated you?"

"I had much rather not."

"Then I think you had better put up at the Golden Lion in High Holborn. It isn't usual for a lady to stay at an inn unattended, but the landlord and his wife were in service with my father for many years, and if you mention my name they will take particular care of you. There will be no need for you to enter the public rooms."

She thanked him again and asked for his address. "So that I can return your generous loan."

He wrote it down for her; she was interested to see that he had a house in Pall Mall, the broad, handsome street that ran between St. James's Palace and the Opera House.

He rose to go, wishing her well in a doubtful tone, as though this might be an error in taste—for what prospect of happiness could there be for a young woman still tied to a husband who had deserted her?

As he reached the door he turned, gave her a long, enigmatic look and said, "I wish we could have met in different circumstances."

Then he was gone.

She felt a curious pang, a sense of loss, but this was no time for repining. Thanks to Hugh Rainham she was free from the threat of the sponging house; she was also free from Carlow and the Chalkeys, she must start planning her own life. The first thing was to find a cheap lodging. She consulted the maid, Sarah, the one person in the house who had not turned against her.

"A lodging, ma'am?" repeated Sarah. "Well, to be sure, there's my sister with a room standing empty this minute, and everything as clean as a new pin. But it's down in Spitalfields—she's married to a silk weaver—hardly the neighbourhood for a lady like yourself."

Rosalba hastily reassured her. Nothing would suit her better. She knew that Sarah's sister would be respectable and that Spitalfields would be cheap, and these were the two conditions she needed while she was looking for work. It seemed like a good omen.

4

Rosalba was transported to Spitalfields by chair, taking all her worldly goods with her. She had to sit with her feet on one bundle and the rest on her knee. It was rather a crush, and even then she was forced to leave her hoop behind, but she was not likely to need it in her new life; ladies in reduced circumstances must make do with reduced petticoats, she decided philosophically.

It was a long way to Spitalfields, a drab working district on the far side of the City towards Bethnal Green. Gazing about her rather fearfully, Rosalba was puzzled at first to make out what was odd about the smoke-stained but solid brick houses crammed into the streets round the market. Until she realized that they each had a row of windows running the whole length of the top story, and so much glass up near the roof gave them a curious, upside-down appearance.

They found the home of Sarah's sister, Mrs. Rougetel, a placid woman who accepted her would-be lodger without question, much to Rosalba's relief, for it could not be every day that ladies from Mayfair moved into this neighborhood, and it was clear that the chairmen thought her a thoroughly fishy customer. She was glad to see the last of them.

"It's a very small room, ma'am," said Mrs. Rougetel.

Which it certainly was—there was hardly space for anything except the bed—but it was neat and clean and beautifully warm, even without a fire, for the kitchen chimney ran up behind one of the walls. As they stood looking round, Rosalba heard strange sounds overhead: a monotonous clacking and the movement of feet, always in the same sequence, rhythmically repeated.

"You can hear them throwing the shuttle," said Mrs. Rougetel. "The loom is up there on the top floor and our whole family works at the silk weaving. The Rougetels are all of that trade; they came over here nigh on seventy years ago, when the French king turned out all the Protestants."

So that accounted for the well-lit upper floor. It was the household workshop. When Rosalba met the weaver at supper she thought that he and two of his four children had a French look about them, dark and sleek, but in speech they were all complete Londoners.

She had told Mrs. Rougetel she was a widow. A married woman living apart from her husband was bound to excite suspicion. She had reverted to her maiden name and now called herself Mrs. York. If the Rougetels got hold of the idea that she had come down here to hide from her dead husband's creditors, they did not seem to think any the worse of her.

Rosalba enjoyed the simple family supper of bacon and pease pudding—it was the first proper meal she had eaten for two days. Afterwards she retired to her little room to think out her strategy for finding work.

Impoverished ladies who had to earn their living generally became governesses or teachers. Unless they went on the stage and became famous actresses. The girl that Rosalba had been six months ago would have rushed hopefully into a theatrical career. It would be much more amusing, and she knew she was pretty enough. Since her marriage she had visited a good many provincial theaters and observed life from the fringes of society, and it had dawned on her that actresses, apart from those at the very peak of the profession, lived equivocal and precarious lives. She would be wiser to try teaching in a school.

She would have to discover a school where they needed an extra teacher, and she soon thought of a way of doing this. She would select a genteel neighbourhood, go into a shop and ask about local seminaries for young ladies; she would pretend she was on her way to visit an imaginary niece and had unfortunately mislaid the address. She was so pleased with this brilliant idea that she slept well and woke in high spirits.

She decided to try her luck in Bloomsbury, which she knew to be a very respectable part of London where many prosperous families lived. It was a long way from Spitalfields, but she did not mind the walk, and the first part of her plan worked admirably. Her air of well-bred innocence was convincing, the story of a lost address was easily believed, and kind people were ready to suggest the names of any number of schools.

It was when she began going round to these addresses that she came up against a difficulty. No one had a vacancy for an additional governess (or perhaps no one wanted an applicant who came unsponsored to the door). At any rate, none of the presiding schoolma'ams would see her. She was politely but firmly turned away.

At last she had to give up and go back to her lodging, tired and disappointed. But she must not give way; she had only to persevere and she was bound to find a post. Next day she was back in Bloomsbury again, trudging wearily down endless streets. She had never seen the outside of so many front doors.

At last she thought the tide was going to turn. A Miss Wendell, who kept a small school in a street off Russell Square, consented to receive her.

She was shown into a dark parlor smelling of beeswax and (for some reason) onions. Miss Wendell was a severe lady in a hideous cap. She did not ask Rosalba to sit down.

"I suppose you have come after Miss Larkin's place. I do not understand how the news got about that she was leaving. However, you may as well give me your credentials. Have you any previous experience of teaching?"

"I'm afraid not, ma'am."

"You look to be about twenty years of age. How have you earned your living until now?"

"I was not obliged to do so until my husband's death. But I have been well educated, at Miss Paley's school in Norwich, and I am sure she would give me a good character. I have studied history, mathematics and French, as well as singing, drawing and painting. I can play the harpsichord and I am thought to write a very good hand."

"You say you are a widow. How long has your husband been dead?"

"Two months, ma'am," said Rosalba, more or less at random, for this was something she had not worked out.

"Then why are you not in mourning?"

Rosalba was silent. The only answer she could think of—that she could not afford to spend money on clothes—would actually have been true if Carlow had died suddenly instead of deserting her, but she realized that this explanation would simply lower her in the eyes of Miss Wendell.

"There is no point in continuing this interview," said the schoolmistress, viewing Rosalba with deep disapproval. "You would not suit. And I may as well warn you, for your own good, that no young person of your appearance and demeanor is likely to be entrusted with the care of sheltered pupils in a select academy such as mine."

Rosalba was ushered out ignominiously into the street.

She stood on the pavement, at a loss. It was no good telling herself that she would have hated working for that gorgon of a woman. Beggars couldn't be choosers, and she would have been thankful for the chance. She hugged her cloak around her, shivering a little. An old man was coming towards her, crying, "Old chairs to mend!" A maid came out of one of the nearby houses, carrying a chair with a broken seat. The old man settled down to work at the edge of the pavement, damping his canes with water from a leather jug, so that he could interlace a taut new pattern across the wide frame of the chair. All this happened while she was standing there, thinking. She had been wasting her time on a wild goose chase. No one would employ her as a teacher. When, by sheer coincidence, she applied at a school where there really was a vacancy, she was rejected as being too young, too inexperienced and perhaps too pretty. She might as well try the stage after all.

Rather doubtingly she set off walking to Covent Garden. It seemed a very long way. She had only just realized how dauntingly large London was. Living pretentiously with Carlow in Mayfair, she had not appreciated the contrast between the spacious gentility of Bloomsbury, the go-ahead bustle of the City and the shabby, workaday region where she was now lodging. The streets around Covent Garden were different again, raffish and rather sinister. There was a reason for this. The tall, narrow, crumbling houses here had been built in the last century and were coming to the end of their leases; most of them had been let very cheaply to disreputable tenants who had turned them into brothels. Rosalba did not know this; she thought the atmosphere of dissolute and seedy festivity must be created by the presence of actors and actresses. Two men accosted her as she hurried along. She ignored them both and was left in peace, but when she came to a halt immediately opposite the Theatre Royal, trying to summon up the courage to go in, she was accosted once again, this time by a young woman.

"Get along with you. This place is taken, see?"

Uncomprehending, Rosalba stared into the painted face of a plump creature upholstered in tarnished finery.

"You heard me!" screamed this vision, when Rosalba did not move. "Try to steal my customers and I'll scratch your eyes out, you simpering doll."

Enlightened, Rosalba stepped back, almost into the arms
35

of an older woman who had come up behind her, to whom she apologized in some confusion.

"It is of no consequence," said the soft-spoken matron, who was expensively dressed and looked most respectable. "But you are not quite at home in these surroundings, my dear young lady. You are from the country, I daresay? If you will come to my house, which is quite close, I will take good care of you. And I can introduce you to some charming company."

It took Rosalba only a few seconds to grasp the meaning of this invitation. Then she turned and fled.

What on earth am I to do? she wondered miserably, as she dragged herself the weary miles back to Spitalfields. Is it my fault that everyone mistakes me for a harlot? I suppose my face is my misfortune. The early winter dusk was closing in with a sharp scurry of rain, and after so much walking she had rubbed a blister on her heel. She was in a deep state of dejection when she limped into the Rougetels' kitchen.

Mrs. Rougetel was there with her eldest daughter, Tabitha.

"You do look tired and wet, ma'am," she exclaimed. "Come and get warm by the fire. Whatever possessed you to stay out on such a day?"

"I've been seeking employment," said Rosalba, peeling off her gloves and moving gratefully near the glowing hearth.

The Rougetels eyed her sympathetically. They did not need to be told that her search had been unsuccessful. They knew all the fears of working people. Although they owned their own loom, they received the spun silk from a wealthy master weaver who had sixty craftsmen under him and regulated their earnings.

"What kind of employment was you after?" inquired Tabitha.

"I thought I might teach in a school." Rosalba preferred not to mention her trip to Covent Garden.

"Could you not set up as a milliner? Being so ladylike and speaking as nicely as you do."

Rosalba was touched by this compliment, which helped to restore her faith in her own appearance, though she saw that Mrs. Rougetel considered her daughter had been rather impertinent.

"I'm afraid I don't sew nearly well enough to be either a milliner or a mantua-maker. I was never much of a needle-woman. It is too provoking, because I can draw and paint quite well. Do you suppose I could color prints?"

Tabitha glanced at her mother. "What about the China-man? He uses females."

"What does he use them for?" asked Rosalba apprehensively.

After her recent encounters her fancy conjured up alarming possibilities.

"Why, to paint his cups and plates, of course."

"But—is he an oriental?"

"Lord love you, no! His name's Joe Sharp and he keeps a china warehouse. That's why they call him the Chinaman."

Mr. Sharp did not own a pottery, they told her. At his warehouse in the City he sold the tea services and ornaments of various English potters, as well as goods imported from the Far East; some of these were plain white porcelain pieces—blanks, they were called—which were decorated on the premises.

The Rougetels knew about the Chinaman because their former lodger's brother worked for him as a painter. Inquiries were made, and the result was that Rosalba started as a china painter the following Monday morning. This was not the kind of profession she had ever expected or imagined. Half a dozen paintresses, as they were called, sat in a lean-to shed at the back of the warehouse, with a hard north light pouring onto the workbench where rows of porcelain pieces were waiting to be adorned. Rosalba was set to painting garlands of leaves on tea bowls. She was very slow at first, to the pitying scorn of the other women, who seemed to resent her voice and manner and probably thought she gave herself airs. However, the Chinaman himself did not harry her; he was a red-faced, practical man with no nonsense about him, but he had inspected some of her sketches and saw that she could be made useful in time.

At the end of her first eleven-hour day she almost fell off her stool with fatigue. She had indigestion from leaning forward so long, as well as a sharp pain at the top of her spine and across to her right shoulder blade. Her feet were like blocks of ice, and the entwined leaves she had been painting floated before her eyes all the way home and even followed her into an exhausted sleep. Next morning she could have wept at the prospect of such another day. Still, she had to work or starve, and she soon began to grow used to the conditions as her young muscles accommodated themselves to the strain. China painting, besides being honest, was quiet and clean, and the other paintresses friendly enough once they got used to her. When Saturday evening came she went back to Spitalfields with the first money she had ever earned and feeling most cheerful at the prospect of a free day on Sunday.

As soon as she reached her little room, she took her precious earnings out of her pocket and placed them in her small box. She had just done this when Tabitha Rougetel stuck her head round the door.

"You've had a caller."

Rosalba stared at her, dumb with astonishment.

"Came this afternoon and said he'd be back later."

"But no one knows where I am! What was he like?"

"Ever such a fine fellow, my mom said. I didn't see him myself," added Tabitha regretfully. "I was up at the loom. Quite the gentleman though, according to Mam. And he described you to the life."

Rosalba began to feel rather sick.

"Did he give his name?"

Tabitha thought a name had been mentioned. Carling or something of the kind.

"Carlow," said Rosalba with a sense of doom.

"That was it—Carlow."

She went away, leaving Rosalba in a state of panic. Carlow had hunted her down and was coming to reclaim her. How was it possible? She thought this out, and decided that if he had hung around discreetly in Half Moon Street, he might have intercepted Mrs. Rougetel's sister, Sarah, and got the truth out of her. Sarah had always had a soft spot for him, in spite of knowing how badly he often behaved. But why should he be looking for me? she wondered. Just for his own brutal pleasure, to give her the beating that Mr. Rainham had frustrated? Or did he think that once she was sufficiently

38

chastened, he could compel her to fall in with his plans for taking money off lecherous dupes?

Rosalba was not staying to find out. She decided to leave the house immediately, taking with her a bundle of all her belongings that she could carry. She had paid the Rougetels in advance, so she owed them nothing, and she hoped to return in a day or two. One of the paintresses had pointed out some lodgings near the warehouse which she had said were safe for solitary women; Rosalba thought she would go there for a bed.

She crept reluctantly out of the warm, cozy haven where the Rougetels had made her so snug. Her stomach yearned for the savory stew she could smell as she passed the kitchen. She was dog-tired and it was raining. The streets down here were very different from those in Mayfair and Bloomsbury with their smooth, stone-laid thoroughfares and raised pavements. Here there were only cobbles, rough and slippery, without even posts and chains to divide the foot passengers from the horse traffic, and though it was now compulsory for a lantern to hang outside every tenth house to light the way, this was not much help. Rosalba trudged along with her head down against the rain. There were few people out on such a night, but presently two figures blocked her path with coarse lip-smackings and whistles.

"Here's a pretty little duckling!"

"Fancy a cuddle, do you, sweetheart?"

"Please let me pass," said Rosalba as firmly as she could manage.

Her eye was on the larger of the two men as he made an amorous lurch towards her, so that she hardly noticed his companion, until he neatly twisted the bundle from under her arm. Then they both made off into the darkness.

"Hi! Come back—come back!" cried Rosalba.

She ran a few steps after them, which was a ridiculous waste of energy, for of course the two thieves had no intention of stopping, and she supposed she ought to be glad they had not hurt her. She hardly cared. She had lost everything, including not only Hugh Rainham's gold but also her own precious earnings—that was the bitterest blow. She could not go back to the Rougetels' for fear of meeting Carlow, she could not go to a strange lodging house because she had no money. Cold and hopeless, she wandered half across the street in a kind of daze, and was nearly knocked down by a carriage coming round the corner. A man leaned out of the window and shouted at her.

Rosalba was terrified. There were very few carriages to be seen in this poor district, and it flashed into her mind that this must be Carlow, returning to look for her.

She took to her heels, diving into the darkness of a nearby alley. Through the clatter of her own footsteps and the thump of her heart she could hear someone running after her.

She slipped and fell on the muddy ground, struggled to her feet and ran on, only to be brought up against a brick wall. There was no way out of the alley; it was a dead end.

And the man behind her was getting closer. Rosalba flung herself against the wall, sobbing.

"My dear girl, what are you running away from?" asked the voice of Hugh Rainham.

5

"What are you doing here?" demanded Rosalba, as soon as she had caught her breath.

"I might ask you the same question."

It was so dark that they could barely see each other. He took her arm and turned her round, beginning to lead her back along the blind alley to the faint lightness of the main road.

"You're soaking wet," he said, feeling her sleeve. "I'm sorry we nearly ran you down, but surely there was no need to go careering off into the gloom? And what are you doing, may I ask, out alone at night, and in such weather?"

"I thought you were my husband."

"Unfortunately not."

That was what she thought he said, though she could not be sure. She had just put her foot in a hole and would have twisted her ankle but for his strong arm supporting her.

40

"Carlow's looking for me. He came to the house where I've been living—"

"No," said Rainham. "It was I who inquired for you, this afternoon. I was on my way back there when I saw you just now."

She stood still, staring up into his strong, shadowed face, for they had now reached the street once more and the nearest lantern seemed brilliant after her excursion into the dark.

"Then why did you say your name was Carlow?"

"I never said anything of the sort. Do get into the carriage."

Rosalba got in automatically, without thinking, and he followed her.

"I can guess what happened," he added. "I said *your* name was Carlow—that is, I asked for you under your married name and had to cover up rather quickly when the good woman let out that you were calling yourself Mrs. York."

"Of course! How stupid of me not to remember that anyone asking for me would use my real name. I suppose I lost my head, because I am so very anxious not to return to my husband, and besides, I could not think of anyone else who might be looking for me—why were you, sir?"

Mr. Rainham leaned forward and gave an order to the coachman. The carriage creaked into motion. He leaned back on the seat beside her.

"Shall we say I was curious to know how my money was being spent? The money I lent you to pay for your journey to Suffolk."

"Oh," said Rosalba uncomfortably. "Are you very angry? I—I'm afraid I was not perfectly truthful when we last met."

"That is one way of putting it," he agreed cordially, "or one might say that you told me a lot of damned lies."

Rosalba found herself trembling in a thoroughly craven manner; recent events had undermined her usually steady nerves.

Somehow he sensed her fear, for he laid a hand on her wrist and said, in a voice warm with compunction, "Please don't be distressed. I did not mean to reproach you. But what possessed you to stay on in London—and in such a district of London, too—alone and unprotected? It was a most fool-

41

hardy thing to do. Those cousins of yours in Suffolk; don't they really exist? Did you make them up?"

"Oh, they exist. But I misled you about my life at the parsonage, out of false pride," she explained rather bitterly, "because I didn't want to seem a more pitiable object than I was already. The Chalkeys never cared for me; they resented having to house and feed me and were only too anxious to be rid of me. In fact I am pretty sure, looking back, that they must have had doubts about Carlow's character, which they chose to ignore when he conveniently proposed to me."

"I see. In that case I quite understand that you should prefer to keep away from them. Surely you might have told me you intended to remain in town? I might have been able to help you."

That is what I was afraid of, thought Rosalba. She could not tell him that she had felt able to take his money only if he believed that she was immediately removing herself beyond his reach. Perhaps he grasped the point, for he went on at once to explain how he had found her.

"I was worried about you. I hoped you might write to tell me you had arrived in Suffolk."

"And to return the money."

"No!" he exclaimed, sounding both hurt and angry. "Can't you forget the money for five minutes?"

"If you wish." She was conscious of being ungracious.

"Two days ago I called at the Golden Lion—the inn I recommended, where I knew you could stay without annoyance. The people there had seen nothing of you. I went round to Half Moon Street; the Stones knew only that you'd gone away in a chair, but that old servant followed me out and told me you were with her sister. She was in quite an agitation, not knowing whether she should betray your confidence. She decided in the end that you ought not to be abandoned to your own devices, and she was right. China painting indeed!"

"At least I can earn my living. Painting china is respectable and clean."

"It is also dull and menial, and you know it. You look worn out."

By now they had reached the environs of Mayfair, so that
42

there were lanterns hanging outside every house. Streams of light flooded in and out of the carriage windows as they moved along the paved street, and they could see each other's faces, both a good deal strained. Rosalba was too tired to argue.

"Where are we going?" she asked.

"To the house in Pall Mall that I share with my sister. Unfortunately she is away from home, or I know she would have been glad to welcome you. As it is, I must ask my housekeeper to look after you. I hope you don't object," he added a trifle anxiously.

Any objection Rosalba might have had to entering a bachelor establishment was counterbalanced by her relief at not having to meet the kind of fashionable, superior female Mr. Rainham's sister was likely to be. She did not feel equal to such an encounter in her bedraggled state, and she was now so tired and hungry that she had become quite passive.

The hall of Mr. Rainham's house was very large and high. Pale blue walls garlanded with rococo plasterwork ran up through the staircase well. There was a butler in attendance and a footman, a great many candles burning. The housekeeper was summoned, a quiet-moving person in a black dress, and through the distance of her own fatigue Rosalba heard her having some sort of conversation with her master.

Then the woman escorted her upstairs to a bedroom where a maid was hastily lighting a fire.

"How unlucky, ma'am," the housekeeper exclaimed, "that you should have had such a nasty spill from your chaise, and on such a stormy night."

So that's what I've had, is it? thought Rosalba. A carriage accident. I mustn't forget.

"And your dress all wet and stained—I will fetch you something of Miss Rainham's to change into."

Rosalba started to protest, feeling this would be a shocking impertinence on her part. Then she stopped, for if Hugh Rainham had made her out to be a family friend, it would seem natural for her to borrow his sister's clothes in an emergency, and too many scruples might sound peculiar. Also she was horrified by the sight of herself in a good looking-glass—there had been no such luxury at the Rougetels'. She was

43

shabby and haggard, and her hair, besides being very untidy, was dull from neglect. She was thankful to wash in hot, soapy water, and she gave her hair a vigorous brushing and combing before putting it up again. She chose the plainest of the three dresses that were brought for her inspection, a soft yellow dimity with a quilted petticoat to match. The dress was rather loose, but the housemaid pinned it for her and helped her to arrange a simple lawn cap on her dark hair. She then descended the imposing staircase and was shown into the library.

Mr. Rainham was standing in front of the fireplace in a mulberry-red coat. He came forward to greet her.

"I hope you found everything you wanted upstairs? Now you must have supper."

There was a table set for two, and a footman was bringing in various covered dishes. Rosalba was by now almost faint with hunger. Rainham sent away the servant, installed her in the chair nearest the fire and gave her a cup of soup, while he helped her to a dish of sweetbreads in a rich sauce. For the next few minutes she was hard put to it to sip and nibble delicately, instead of devouring her food like a wolf.

Presently she was able to look round at the handsome bookcases with carved pediments, all containing shelves of books identically bound in morocco and probably, she thought, with his family crest stamped in gold on the front.

"You must have a great many volumes here, sir."

"I'm an incurable book-buyer." He leaned across to fill her glass. "I hope you can drink claret? Good. I know it's not a lady's wine, but I thought it would revive you."

It was not until they had finished eating and drinking, and the footman had removed all traces of their meal, that Hugh Rainham raised the subject that was on both their minds: what was to become of Rosalba now?

"Do you mind telling me what you were doing in that china warehouse? Yes, I know you are obliged to support yourself by your own efforts, but there are ways and ways; were you not able to find anything more suitable?"

"It isn't easy for a woman in my position to find genteel employment. I thought I might teach, but no one would take me on."

"Would you like to teach?"

"Not very much," she admitted frankly. "It might prove even more exhausting than painting china. But it would be better than starving. Or joining the only other profession that seems open to me."

He threw her a keen glance, and said in an unexpectedly harsh voice, "Don't talk in that way. It is not at all amusing."

"I assure you, Mr. Rainham, I am deadly serious."

He got up and began to stir the fire with a kind of suppressed violence. She was aware that the idea of her selling her body disturbed and perhaps tormented him. Probably it reminded him of the night he had broken open her door and thought she was seducing his stupid cousin. She ought not to have spoken as she had—yet some dangerous impulse had made her want to provoke him.

Coming back to his chair, Rainham said, "We shall have to consult my sister. She will be back here on Tuesday, and she has so many women friends, I'm sure that one or other of them must require a companion. Don't look so incredulous. There are plenty of families where a well-bred active young woman is needed to help the household run smoothly, make herself useful to an invalid or go about with the unmarried daughters. Olivia is sure to have some suggestions."

Rosalba continued to look and feel incredulous. She already knew, what he might not have realized, that most women did not want dependents who looked like her. On the other hand, the Rainhams moved in a plane of society she had no experience of (she had understood this much more clearly since entering his house) and perhaps among their grand friends there might really be a place where she could be inconspicuous and useful.

So she said meekly, "I daresay I shall become quite proficient at winding wool and walking the pug."

"I must say, it does seem a terrible waste."

He looked straight across at her, his eyes clear and challenging, and Rosalba was paid out for provoking him, because she herself felt a physical pain she had never known before, a pain of intolerable longing. If they gazed at each other for another instant she would be lost.

Then Rainham got up and said formally, "I hope you don't

object to spending the night in this house. I really think it is too late and too stormy for you to leave, and I know you must be very tired. Tomorrow I propose taking you to that inn I told you of, the Golden Lion, where you can stay in seclusion until I am able to consult my sister."

"You are very kind to take so much trouble," said Rosalba.

It was true that she felt too weary to make another move that night; she also knew that he would not have found it necessary to make this speech half an hour ago. After a period of friendliness and ease they had become curiously wary of each other.

She had got into bed between the deliciously smooth linen sheets and blown out the candle when she was seized with the notion that perhaps she ought to lock the door. In case he came trying to make love to her in the night; she didn't want to take any risks. But then suppose he didn't come; if she overslept, the housemaid would find the door locked and all the servants would know that she distrusted him. Which would be a poor repayment for his undemanding generosity. She was still debating this point with herself when she fell asleep. She lay all night in a dreamless coma, her virtue unassailed.

6

Hugh Rainham delivered Rosalba at the Golden Lion, driving with her through a Sunday-morning London which reverberated with the ringing of church bells that pealed to each other from spire to spire across the decorous Sabbath streets.

Arrangements were made with the landlord and his wife: Mrs. York was to have the best room in the house, with her meals served to her there, and access to a private stair, so that she would have no contact with the ordinary patrons of the inn. He parted from her with a rather guarded formality, promising to let her know as soon as he had seen his sister, who was at present visiting friends in Surrey.

He then took himself to his cousin Gus's house in Grosvenor Street and escorted his cousin's wife, Alicia, to morning service at the Grosvenor Chapel. He had known she would not care to go by herself, and he had also known, with the certainty of long experience, that Gus would be in a drunken slumber, impossible to rouse for churchgoing.

By the time Hugh got back to his own house, he found cloaks and cloak bags in the hall and all the signs of a recent arrival.

"What's this, Thompson?" he asked the butler. "Has Miss Rainham come home?"

"Yes, sir! I understand that Mrs. Falconer received an express last night, saying that her father has been taken seriously ill. Mr. and Mrs. Falconer decided to drive up to London first thing this morning and brought Miss Rainham with them."

Rainham ran up the stairs to his sister's apartment on the first floor. He tapped on the door of the dressing room she used as a boudoir and went in.

"So your visit has ended unexpectedly, my dear. I am sorry to hear about Mary Falconer's father, but I hope they will find the news is not so grave as they feared. And I am glad to have you home."

"Are you?" retorted Olivia Rainham in a flat unconciliating voice.

She was a tall woman of twenty-eight, a little too large for beauty. In another walk of life she might have been called a strapping wench; as it was, she had been described as statuesque. She was always immaculately dressed and generally had a confident open expression, though today she seemed somewhat ruffled.

"Is anything the matter?" inquired her brother, with a first prickle of apprehension.

"Oh, nothing. Nothing in the world. To be sure, it would have been a trifle awkward if I'd come home last night to find you disporting yourself with your latest fancy piece. How you could bring such a person into my home, Hugh! I don't attempt to judge you for anything you do elsewhere, but to let that creature spend the night here and wear my clothes—"

"The lady who stayed here last night is not my mistress. She is a very unfortunate victim of circumstance—"

"*Lady,*" repeated Olivia in tones of scorn and loathing.

47

"How can you be so deceitful? I know who she was—that immoral hussy who has been living with Ben Robinson's card-playing crony, the people who tried to extort money out of Gus. She should have been whipped and put in the stocks."

"You don't know what you are talking about," said Hugh, his voice cold with anger.

"Oh yes, I do! I suppose you didn't realize that Gus's groom was round here last night, visiting our servants, and he recognized your innocent victim when she arrived, looking like a streetwalker, he said. Temperance has been telling me all about it."

Temperance was the second housemaid, a sanctimonious woman he had always disliked.

He said austerely that Olivia ought to know better than to gossip with the servants, and set about trying to correct her bad opinion of Rosalba. Olivia had always been a great champion of her own sex; she often assisted women in difficulties, even women who had brought disgrace on themselves by running away from home or having unauthorized babies. He had forgotten, when thinking that she would help Rosalba, that her protegées generally came from a lower rank in society and had always been impeccably virtuous before their fall from grace. Pretty Rosalba, living in apparent complicity with her villainous husband, had created a dubious impression—he had misjudged her himself, as he now had to explain. But the more he tried to reason with Olivia, the more convinced she was of Rosalba's total depravity.

She was proud of her brother, inclined to be possessive about him. If he could be so taken in by that dreadful woman, he must be utterly infatuated. This upset Olivia, and her hostility became exaggerated.

"I shall never be able to bear the sight of my favorite yellow dress again, after that slut wore it. I shall tell them to burn it. And the sheets that were on her bed."

(She did not mean this but it sounded effective.)

"If that is the kind of hysterical nonsense you are going to talk, there is no point in my listening to you," said Hugh, turning away in disgust.

"Where are you going?"

"Out," he replied noncommittally.

In fact he was going back to the Golden Lion.

Rosalba had spent the middle part of the day luxuriating in a comfortable chair in front of a crackling fire. She knew she had only to pick up a small brass bell to summon pots of tea or coffee or anything else she wanted. She had plenty to read, for Mr. Rainham had lent her several books from his library—and they did have his crest on the front: a stag passant surmounting the word "Fidele." She was hesitating between *Tristram Shandy* and a volume of foreign travels when the owner of the books walked in unannounced.

"I did not expect to see you again so soon, Mr. Rainham," she said, trying not to sound too pleased. Then she saw his expression. "Is anything wrong?"

"I'm afraid I have been very stupid, raised hopes that I cannot fulfill. My sister arrived home this morning—"

Rosalba grasped the point at once. "She disapproves—doesn't want to have anything to do with me."

"I'm sorry," he said almost humbly. "I never thought she would be so narrow-minded."

"Oh well, I shall have to abandon the career of a genteel companion. I daresay I should have wound the wool round the pug."

While she pretended to laugh, she thought, I shall have to go back to Spitalfields and the china warehouse. During that strange period, just under a fortnight, since Carlow deserted her, she had never faced the full desolation of her future life stretching endlessly ahead. At first she had been too frightened of not being able to survive, and then, after she found work, too exhausted. She had hardly been aware of her own isolation and loneliness, without a friend of her own kind, drudging all day and collapsing into her little room at night, with no hope of variation, nothing better to look forward to.

Now, after a few hours' escape in the company of Hugh Rainham, the bleakness of despair came over her and the tears began to slide silently down her cheeks.

"I have made you so unhappy," he said with an anguish as great as her own.

Rosalba had a useful gift, though she was quite unaware of it, of remaining beautiful even when she cried. The tears clung to her long eyelashes and glittered like diamonds before they fell. Hugh watched her, fascinated.

After a moment he reached out a tentative hand and touched her shoulder.

"This is all my fault."

"I don't see how you can think that."

"Olivia has formed a completely false impression of you. Which need never have happened if I had brought you straight here, instead of stupidly asking you to stay the night."

"Oh, is that what she finds so shocking? It seems a pity we both behaved so well."

She had spoken incautiously, trying to overcome her self-pity, which clearly distressed him. There was a moment while they gazed at each other and she felt his fingers tightening and a current of excitement passing through to her.

"Do you mean that?" he asked.

"Yes," said Rosalba, certain that she did mean it.

He bent down to kiss her mouth, then he lifted her out of the chair and carried her to the bed. From the first instant she responded with a passionate enjoyment. Her senses seemed to flower and expand. She had never known it was possible to feel as she did now, and still did not realize how much her astonishment told him.

"This has never happened to you before, has it, my treasure?" he asked presently.

"I've been married six months," she reminded him.

"Married perhaps. But never loved."

"And never in love until I met you," she whispered indelicately now, and reaching up to hold him even closer.

The room was growing dim and cold when Rainham got up to light the candles and shovel some coal on the fire. Then he came back to sit on the bed beside her.

"We have a lot to talk about, my dear. We must make plans. But first of all, do tell me what your name is—it seems quite absurd, but I don't know it."

"I am called Rosalba."

"Rosalba York? That is a charming fancy, but I meant your true name."

"That is my true name. At least, it was until I married.

My maiden name was York, and my parents christened me Rosalba. Did you think I was silly enough to make it up?"

"No, no!" he said, laughing. "I see I have offended you. It was your parents who were fanciful—but much more successful than most of the givers of romantic names to squalling infants. My exquisite white rose."

"What am I to call you, Mr. Rainham?"

"Certainly not that," he replied, looking thunderstruck.

"It does not sound stiff, but simply to say Rainham reminds me of your stupid cousin. Only because I met him first," she added hastily, seeing his eyebrows crease together over the senatorial nose in an alarming fashion.

"One would not wish to remind anyone of Gus. You had better call me Hugh."

"Hugh," she repeated shyly.

Using his Christian name gave her an almost greater sense of intimacy than making love.

He said, "I can see there is only one person whose companion you ought to be. Mine. If I take a house for you, will you come and live in it and make me happy?"

"Oh, how I should like to," she exclaimed impulsively. Then her delight was clouded. "It would not be right, would it? I ought not to become—a kept woman."

He took her hand gently, and asked, "Are you very religious?"

"No."

She had been as a girl, but two years with the Chalkeys at the parsonage, she thought, had cured her of that.

"So it is not our living in sin that would trouble you, so much as your living at my expense?"

"I'm not sure. Yes. I suppose so," admitted Rosalba, who was in no state to analyze her scruples.

She knew that what he was suggesting was wrong; you did not have to be *very* religious to appreciate that.

"I know it's not a perfect solution," said Hugh. "But what else are we to do? You're tied to that scoundrel and he's left you entirely unprovided for. I can't ask you to live with me in my own house, on account of my sister, and anyway your position would be just as awkward there. Are you suggesting that you should go back to the Chinaman on weekdays and that I should collect you in the carriage every Sunday? That would not be very amusing for either of us."

Rosalba shook her head and gazed at him beseechingly. She had caught a note of impatient sarcasm.

"Then I can see no alternative. You aren't going to run away from me, are you, my love? Just after we've found each other."

"Oh no—I could not bear to do that!"

She had not put up much of a struggle. Perhaps all her capacity for struggling had been worn out in the efforts of the past fortnight. By the time she and Hugh were dressed once more, and he had rung the bell and ordered dinner for them both, she had agreed to live with him openly as his mistress.

They made plans. Rosalba must write and tell the Rougetels that she was going to live with friends who had offered her a home. Hugh suggested that she should send them an extra week's rent to compensate for her sudden departure. In the meantime, she could stay here quietly until he had found her a house.

He soon fixed on one, just inside the parish of Soho, where it bordered on Mayfair. Hunsden Street led nowhere in particular, it was quiet and secluded, containing no more than thirty small houses, built at the beginning of the century. Number 17 had been painted recently, which was an advantage. The ground floor comprised a good little square hall, more impressive than a mere passage, and a parlor for meals. Above there was a miniature but perfectly proportioned drawing room, one bedroom and a dressing room. There was an attic overhead and a basement where the kitchen, larder and pantry were neatly fitted in.

"How charming it is!" said Rosalba, walking about the uncarpeted drawing room in an ecstasy of admiration. "How soon can I move in?"

"As soon as we have it furnished. And you will need some servants, of course."

"Oh dear. I know one must have servants; the thing is, I have never employed any before and I don't know how I should set about engaging them."

"You need do nothing. I'll speak to Thompson; he'll see to everything."

"But—won't he object?"

"What about?" Hugh was genuinely puzzled. "Oh, I see what you mean. No, he won't object, and if he did, he would not be the sort of man I should care to employ as my butler. It's not his business to criticize the way I choose to arrange my life. And by the way, he will choose the kind of servants who will treat you with proper respect."

They decided on a bed, with a rose-colored canopy and window curtains to match, and chose a great many other things besides, including a sofa upholstered in green velvet, a pier glass in a gilded frame, a silver coffeepot, a harpsichord and an exotic-looking tea service, though not from the china warehouse where Rosalba had been working.

He also encouraged her to choose a great many new clothes. She felt more uncomfortable about this than she did about the house furnishings, which she still thought of as really belonging to him. Clothes were different. Yet how could she regard them as the wages of sin? It was impossible to associate the earning of wages with anything she enjoyed so much as making love with Hugh!

The furniture arrived at 7 Hunsden Street and three servants were installed: a cook, a housemaid who was also capable of acting as Rosalba's dresser, and a not-too-grand footman who was prepared to do various menial jobs for the little household before donning his striped waistcoat and fancy jacket.

On the very evening of the day she moved in, Hugh took Rosalba to a party. Miss Priscilla Denny lived near Hanover Square, in a house provided for her by the Earl of Retford. When Rosalba climbed the stairs beside her lover and moved toward a room that was sparkling with lights and voices, she felt extremely nervous. She had no idea what kind of a society she would be stepping into as she passed through those doors, openly proclaiming herself as a woman of pleasure, the kept mistress of a wealthy man. It was true that she was treated with civility by tradesmen and servants who were well aware of her position, but the people here had nothing to lose by showing their contempt. The men, at any rate, must despise her, and if most of the women were in the same boat as herself, that was no consolation, for she was afraid they would be brazen, flaunting creatures, predatory and spiteful. And might there not be a kind of behavior she was not used to? Stories flitted through her mind of shameless females dancing on tables....

Their hostess came forward to meet them. She was about twenty-two years old and very fair; her white-and-silver dress was a miracle of elegant simplicity.

"I am very happy to meet you, ma'am," she said to Rosalba in a cool but perfectly amiable voice. "I believe you are just settling into your new house. May I call on you in a day or two?"

"By all means, ma'am. I should be delighted."

A middle-aged man with a clever, lined face said to Hugh in an undertone, "Congratulations, my dear fellow. What a dark horse you are."

Hugh said, "Mrs. York, may I present Lord Retford."

"How do you do, Mrs. York." Retford studied her with some curiosity, but without, she thought, any hint of the lecherous inclination she had half dreaded in her new situation. "All is now explained. We have been quite anxious about poor Rainham, you know. He has not been at all himself these last ten days, able to talk of nothing but leases and linen drapers and the best place to buy coal."

"No—has he, my lord!" said Rosalba, surprised out of her shyness. "How very odd!"

She stood beside Hugh in her beautiful new hooped dress of apple-green silk, her petticoat embroidered with tiny flowers, her hair piled up in a white cloud, and felt him smiling down at her.

After this it was possible to take in the other guests. The men all seemed very agreeable, not noticeably rakish, and a good deal more presentable than most of the men she had met with Carlow. Most of the women were extremely pretty—that was to be expected—and no more heavily painted than the current fashion allowed. Their public deportment was not at all unseemly, and they dressed in a very good style. The only one whose appearance might have been called vulgar turned out to be the blameless wife of a rising playwright.

Rosalba was intrigued by a couple who arrived together, rather late. The woman was tall and graceful; the delicate beauty of her features and her alabaster complexion might be too subtle for some tastes, but there was an extraordinary sweetness in her glance and a touch of sadness too that made her a little remote. Her companion was quite simply the handsomest man Rosalba had ever seen. Even in the dizzy raptures of her love for Hugh, she could see he was surpassed, in looks if nothing else, by this superb Adonis.

When supper was served, Hugh took her to join this romantic pair and introduced them.

"My dear Margaret, you said you would like to meet Mrs. York. Rosalba, this is Mrs. Lodney, who has known me nearly all my life. And Mr. St. John Roche."

Margaret Lodney smiled at Rosalba and said, "How delightful it is to make your acquaintance. In fact, it is my reward for coming here this evening. I don't go to parties as a rule."

As she murmured some sort of answer, Rosalba heard Mr. Roche say to Hugh, "I nearly had to drag her here by force. I told her she would enjoy it if she came."

"Well, you were right," said Mrs. Lodney, "though I hope I should have had the courtesy to come in any case. I could not refuse Priscilla, when she and Retford have been so kind to me."

"Kind!" exploded Roche. "What is so particularly kind about ordinary friendliness and good manners? Of all the destructive emotions, I think gratitude is the greatest millstone. Don't you agree, Mrs. York?"

Rosalba did not know how to reply. Her own intense gratitude to Hugh did not seem to plant any difficulties in the progress of their love. On the other hand, when she thought of the Chalkeys, she remembered how very much she had resented being grateful to them. And neither of these responses could be cited while Mrs. Lodney and Mr. Roche were having a private argument which she could not follow. Again she murmured something noncommittal, and was relieved when they were interrupted by a footman filling their wineglasses.

Later, when she and Hugh were back in Hunsden Street, she asked him about Mrs. Lodney.

"What is her history? And how is it you have known her for so long?"

"She used to be a childhood friend of my sister's. She married a man called George Lodney with a place in Rutland, a London house, a large fortune—two years ago she threw up everything and ran away with St. John Roche."

He paused. Rosalba did not speak.

"There was a devil of a scandal," he continued. "Margaret's family tried to bring her back and patch things up, but she wouldn't come, and in the end Lodney divorced her. She and Roche are now living a few miles from the center of the world she was born into, and from which she has become an outcast. None of her former women friends can meet her, and she has no hope of being received in their houses."

It was unnecessary to add that before her elopement Margaret Lodney would never have set foot in the house of a woman like Priscilla Denny. Gentlemen might move freely from one world to the other; ladies could not.

"I am very sorry for Margaret," said Hugh, taking Rosalba's hand. "When I asked you to come and live with me, my love, it came into my calculations that you would not have to suffer much from that kind of exclusion. Your relations had treated you so abominably that you were already alone in the world, and you had no friends in London to cut you dead. If I'd been in Roche's place, I think I'd have taken Margaret further afield than Westminster. Although he loves her, he is apt to be obtuse and a little selfish."

"He has not seen fit to marry her."

Rosalba knew that men did not usually marry their mistresses, but in these circumstances she thought it would have been considered the proper thing for him to do.

"That is not his fault. I'm sure he intended to marry her. When the divorce went through—you know it has to be done by a special Act of Parliament—our noble legislators were in a moralizing mood and they made it a condition that Margaret should not be allowed to marry again. As a warning to any other wives who contemplated running away."

"Oh, that was cruel!"

"It can't have made much difference. As a divorced woman,

she could never have been received in society, even if she remarried."

But at least she would have been sure of Roche, thought Rosalba. As it was, it would be possible for him to abandon her at some time in the future and marry someone else. The implications sent a shiver of panic through her. Suddenly their bright little house had become cold with foreboding.

7

"I shall have to leave you for a few days at Christmas, my love," said Hugh regretfully. "I have promised to go down to Sussex. I wish I need not, but it is a long-standing plan and I cannot cry off."

Rosalba's heart sank. This was what she had dreaded from the start: being left alone while he pursued his other life elsewhere. But she had known how it must be; she would not humiliate herself or irritate him by making a fuss.

So she smiled and said cheerfully, "Will you be joining your sister?"

"No, I am going to the Talmarshes, very old friends. Olivia has taken herself off to Derbyshire. I seem to be in her black books—I can't think why."

They both laughed, for they knew perfectly well why. Olivia had not forgiven him for his public liaison with Rosalba.

By the time he went to Sussex, Rosalba had some engagements of her own. She had been invited to dine on Christmas Day with Mrs. Palmer, a well-known actress she had met at Priscilla Denny's, and no sooner had she accepted than a note came from Margaret Lodney asking her to spend a few days at their house near Westminster. On Christmas morning she went to the nearest church, sitting right at the back in a dark place under the gallery and slipping out before the Communion. She walked round to Soho Square, feeling dispirited, but the house was so full of theater people, musicians, painters and above all children that it was impossible not to enjoy the jolly friendliness, hot fires, good food and drink.

Rosalba had a far pleasanter Christmas than the last two, which she had spent with the Chalkeys.

The next day a carriage came to fetch her to Walton Lodge. Margaret Lodney and St. John Roche lived in almost rural seclusion tucked away beyond Buckingham House and the Royal Parks, in a side turning off the King's Road. It must be sufficiently isolated, Rosalba thought, for her to hide in, while close enough for him still to reach all the haunts of a man of fashion: the clubs, theaters, coffee houses, even the aristocratic homes, from which a scandalous elopement had not excluded him. The villa itself was charming, light and spacious; no expense had been spared. Her host and hostess were in the breakfast room when she arrived, and she joined them for a cup of coffee. Margaret wanted to know about her dinner in Soho Square.

"Was the house crammed with all those conceited actors, talking at the tops of their voices about things one doesn't understand?"

"Yes, but I found that rather interesting. There were other things talked of too, and we had a great many games to divert the children. Mrs. Palmer is a very good mother, I think."

Margaret drew a sharp breath, and Roche interrupted almost rudely, asking some question about the drive. Rosalba was struck by an appalling thought. When Margaret ran away from her husband had she also deserted a young family? Fearing the worst, she floundered through a description of an overturned chaise at Hyde Park Corner.

Margaret got up and left the room.

Rosalba appealed to Roche. "I am afraid I have been dreadfully thoughtless and clumsy. I suppose I should not have mentioned children. Are there—has she—"

"Two boys and a girl, the youngest not three years old," he said gloomily. "She has lost them forever, and it is on my account."

"Surely Mrs. Lodney does not tell you that?"

"No, never. She takes all the blame on herself. But it is not very agreeable to be the object for whom so much has been sacrificed. I sometimes feel as though I had been rescued from a burning building in which others, far worthier, had been left to perish."

Rosalba felt sorry for him but could think of no consolation.

When Margaret came back, she was very bright and scintillating. She showed the visitor all round the house and garden, and talked of music and books almost without drawing breath. Gradually this frentic liveliness calmed down into something more natural, though she was never entirely off her guard. Watching her with Roche, Rosalba thought they must consider their elopement had been worth the price they were both paying, for they appeared to be completely besotted. It seemed astonishing that a woman with as much sensibility as Margaret would behave as she did in front of a third person: following Roche about with spaniel eyes, positively encouraging him to fondle and caress her. I shouldn't want Hugh to treat me like that if there was someone looking on, she decided. But the mere thought of Hugh became almost intolerable while she was playing gooseberry to this amorous couple, and at the end of the week she was glad enough to go back to Soho, where she occupied herself in moving the furniture about, teaching the cook to make a very special syllabub and playing the harpsichord. She was sadly out of practice.

She was wrestling so intently one afternoon with a piece by J. C. Bach that she did not hear the sounds of someone arriving in the hall, or even the quick footsteps on the stair.

"Bravo!" said a voice behind her. "I'd no idea you were such an accomplished performer."

Hugh was standing in the doorway, still in his greatcoat. She ran into his arms.

"Oh, how glad I am to see you! I didn't expect you for another week. But how cold you are, my love."

"I couldn't stay away any longer. I missed you too much."

"And the ground was too hard for hunting," observed Rosalba, who was after all a country-bred girl.

He laughed. "That also. But I kept seeing you in my mind's eye and wondering what you were doing every hour of the day."

She found to her great delight that he meant to come and stay with her at Hunsden Street for the time being, London—his London—being so depleted of company at present that the house in Pall Mall could stand empty, while they remained together in their private Eden.

"We may as well make the most of it," he said, "for once people come back to town, you will have plenty of callers and you will have to start entertaining a little. A card party, perhaps."

Rosalba made a face.

"Have you an absolute aversion to that?" he asked. "I know you have some reason, but everybody plays, and it is rather difficult to receive company in a house as small as this without resort to cards."

"Yes, I know I must play. Only I am not very good. I'd much rather play chess."

Next day Hugh went round to his house in Pall Mall and came back with an elegantly inlaid games table and a set of chessmen. After dinner they sat down to play.

"I'll give you a pawn," he told her kindly.

"Thank you."

The game progressed in silence for some time, to the companionable ticking of the bracket clock. After a longish pause Rosalba made an apparently random move with one of her knights.

Hugh said, "Would you like to go back and have that move again?"

"I don't think so."

"Very well, my love. On your head be it."

He brought up a bishop and the knight was swept away.

"Check," said Rosalba gently.

"What?"

He looked again and saw that he had walked into a neat trap. By moving his bishop he had exposed his king to her castle. From then on he was on the defensive. About ten minutes later he conceded victory.

"I wasn't attending properly," he said in a somewhat lofty manner.

"And you did give me a pawn," said Rosalba, very demure.

She thought he was annoyed at being defeated by a woman. Then he laughed.

"Who taught you to play, you little sorceress?"

"My father, during his last illness."

"Childhood is the time to learn. We'll start as equals in future."

This momentous chess game had another equalizing effect. From now on he began to talk to her about politics, science and other serious topics he had hardly mentioned to her before. He was not at all condescending, but rather touchingly pleased that she should be willing to share his interests.

It was very snug in Hunsden Street. They were having a hard winter, never more than a powdering of snow with sharp frosts every night, and the Thames was frozen in places. Though the ice on the river was not strong enough to bear, there was plenty of skating on lakes and ponds.

"I should like to skate," said Rosalba, lying in bed one morning and gazing at the opaque white window engraved all over with lines as fine as the cotton-twist filaments in the stem of a wineglass.

"Can you do that too?" inquired Hugh, pulling her down under the quilt. "What a talented creature you are—a skating chessplayer, the wonder of the age!"

"If you are going to be impertinent I shan't stay in bed with you a minute longer."

"Oh yes, you will, my girl!"

Rational conversation came to an end for the time being; there was a good deal of activity and laughter.

Presently he said, "If you'd like to skate, we'll make an expedition. The roads are not too bad, and it will do the horses good to have some exercise."

Immediately after breakfast his carriage was summoned from the mews, a hamper of food was packed, two pairs of bone skates obtained from somewhere—one of the remarkable things about Hugh was his ability to produce whatever was wanted at a moment's notice; this was probably due to his having a wide experience of the world and a great deal of money, but it seemed like magic. They started off from Hunsden Street, Rosalba with a hot brick at her feet and her hands in a fur muff.

"Where are we going?" she inquired.

"To the Nabob's Vineyard."

"Good gracious, where is that?"

"At Liston Farley, not far from Uxbridge."

61

"Why do you call it the Nabob's Vineyard?"

"Because it was built by my Uncle Theodore, who was a nabob and who wanted to excite the envy of all his relations. You don't know much about my family, do you?"

She shook her head. She had wanted to know but had somehow felt it was not her place to ask.

Hugh settled back in the carriage and stretched his long legs.

"The Rainhams have owned a house in Derbyshire called Ashwin since the Middle Ages. I am prejudiced, but I think it is the most beautiful house I know. It has descended in the male line through an entail for sixteen generations. My grandfather had four sons. John was the heir; his path was marked out for him. Robert went into the army and became a general. He is the only one of the brothers still alive. He and his wife live in a family house a few miles from Ashwin and have two surviving children, my young cousins William and Lettice. My father married an heiress; he was taken care of. That sounds a trifle heartless, but it was a marriage of affection; he was devoted to my mother. Something had to be done with Theodore. He was a young scapegrace, so he was packed off to India. He came home twenty years later with a large fortune—one does not inquire too minutely into how he got it—and proceeded to build himself a house which was to make all the other Rainham possessions look paltry. I think he was one of those men who must always have a grudge of some sort and are trying to get their own back."

"How did his brothers take it?"

"My father and my Uncle Robert were more amused than annoyed. Sir John had come into the baronetcy by then; he had a silly, extravagant, ambitious wife and they were short of money. They goaded Uncle Theodore so assiduously that everything he had went to them and afterwards to their son, Gus. His parents could never face the fact that their only child, the heir to all this splendor, was born with a weak character and a vacant head. Instead of trying to shore him up against these misfortunes, they spoiled and indulged him and made him quite unbearable. Perhaps it is just as well they are both dead, for even they could hardly deceive themselves any longer."

He sounded bitter. She studied him curiously. He met her glance and flushed slightly.

"It sounds as though I am the one most afflicted by envy, doesn't it? I admit I do envy Gus one thing which he doesn't want and I can never possess. Ashwin itself."

"The beautiful house?"

"Yes. You see, he doesn't care about the place, never lived there as a child, as I did, and he neglects it shockingly. When a building stands empty for a few years the damp starts to get in, and this is what has happened at Ashwin. Gus will do nothing to preserve the plaster ceilings or the family portraits, won't even have the roof repaired."

"Why ever not?"

"I think he resents the house's existence. He can't sell it because of the entail. He doesn't want to live there, has no taste for country life and no interest in history. And he won't spend money on anything that isn't going to produce some immediate gratification for himself."

"This other house we're going to, that's in the country."

"An hour's drive from town; he can use it to give parties, to bolster up his own consequence, and hurry back to his natural haunts directly the silence becomes too much for him. He isn't there at present, by the way. Alicia is expecting a child and they are to remain with her father in Hampshire for the time being. Lord Petersfield doesn't want his daughter worrying herself into a fever over the kind of antics Gus gets up to when he is in town."

By now they had reached the imposing gates of Liston Farley. The carriage turned in to the park. They came almost at once to the lake, and behind it on rising ground they saw the nabob's mansion. A classical facade of orange brick was perhaps a little too bright for the muted pastel colors of winter that filled the rest of the landscape. The carriage stopped and they got out. Hugh told the coachman to drive on to the house and ask that a fire should be lit in one of the rooms and the picnic hamper taken in to wait for them.

There was a rustic seat beside the lake. Rosalba sat on it while Hugh fastened on their skates. Then he led her onto the ice. It was several years since she had been on skates, but it was a skill never forgotten. As she and Hugh crossed hands and kicked away from the bank, she felt a wonderful exhilaration. She had pinned up her skirt beforehand to shorten it a good six inches, and her hip-length cape of scarlet wool, called a polonaise, swung out behind her as though she had wings. They swooped over the breadth of the lake; the speed and rhythm, the dazzling cold air on her cheeks and in her lungs made her almost dizzy with excitement. Faster and faster they raced along, until she had a stitch and cried out for him to stop.

"Hugh—I can't—"

He turned his foot inward; the pace dwindled and came to a halt. They stood laughing into each other's eyes.

"Did you enjoy that?"

"Oh yes!"

They both knew this shared physical pleasure had been somehow akin to a consummation of love.

They skated on more sedately now, until Rosalba's ankles began to ache and Hugh said they would go indoors and eat their luncheon.

The main entrance to the house was on the other side, but approaching the south front across the grass they came to a short flight of steps with a glass door at the top. Rosalba ran up the steps to peep inside and found the door would open.

"Careless," said Hugh critically.

She felt this was another point against Gus and even the Nabob. The servants at Liston Farley didn't lock up properly.

They stepped into a kind of loggia or secondary hall, with doors leading off in every direction. The doors were of solid mahogany, cased in pillars and pediments of gilded plaster.

"Come into the library," said Hugh, opening one of them. "They've made up a good fire for us, I see. You can wait here, my love, while I find out what's happened to our hamper."

The library was a long narrow room, furnished in varying shades of green. The tightly packed books on the open shelves had an air of immobility, as though they were never taken out and read, unlike the books in Hugh's library in Pall Mall. All the same, thought Rosalba, as she sat down by the fire, the room had quite a lived-in feeling, and she noticed a newspaper dropped by one of the chairs and a bureau with some letters laying on it. She was just thinking that this was rather odd, for the house was supposed to be empty, when the door opened again and three people came in together: a tall, dark woman of about thirty, a very young girl and someone Rosalba recognized instantly, though she had seen her only once, for she was the slightly insipid female who had been talking to Hugh at the moment when Rosalba herself first set eyes on him—Lady Alicia Rainham, Gus's wife, now nearing the end of her pregnancy.

Rosalba jumped to her feet, guilty and confused. They saw her and seemed a little surprised, but not unduly.

The tall woman smiled graciously. "My dear Miss Runcival, we had no idea you had arrived. Why did no one tell us? William thought you would not be with us for another half hour."

This was horribly awkward. It was clear that they took her for another visitor, unknown but expected. She tried to make some demur and was annoyed to find that her voice had dried up in her throat, probably from panic. In the meantime the tall woman was settling Lady Alicia on a sofa and directing the girl, whose name was Lettice, to altar the position of the pole screen so that the heat of the fire should not burn her skin.

Lettice and William, thought Rosalba; they were two of Hugh's cousins, the children of his uncle the general. At last she found her tongue.

"I am afraid there is a mistake. I am not Miss—the lady you were expecting."

Three pairs of eyes surveyed her, astonished but not unfriendly.

"Then who are you?" asked Lettice.

At that moment Hugh came back. He stood transfixed; the ladies gazed at him and then at Rosalba.

"Hugh!" exclaimed the tall one. "When did you arrive, and who is—Oh no! How could you do such a thing? It is too bad of you!"

"Good morning, Olivia," said Hugh, assuming a poise he probably did not feel. "My dear Alicia, how do you do? And why are you not in Hampshire? Where is Gus? He had no business to drag you about the country in this weather."

"I am perfectly well, cousin," said Lady Alicia in a soft,

wavering voice. "Only Gus had a little disagreement with Papa, and he thought it better we should return here."

"Never mind that now," interrupted Miss Olivia Rainham. "I am astounded, Hugh, that you can find time to criticize Gus when you yourself have been guilty of such a horrible inpropriety, bringing that *creature* into a house where she can contaminate innocent members of your own family."

"You had better hold your tongue, Olivia," said Hugh in a steely voice. "You must know very well that I should never have brought Mrs. York to Liston if I had guessed that you would be here to insult her."

He went on to say a good deal more, but Rosalba did not stay to listen. She stood up. Her ankles ached already from the skating, and now she felt as though her legs were stuffed with feathers. It was an effort to cross the library with a steady step and a manner of calm indifference. Lettice held open the door for her. She was a pretty little fair-haired girl, and her eyes were brimming with a sympathetic curiosity, just as galling in its way as active dislike.

Out in the loggia Rosalba did not know which way to go. She was frightened to open any of these forbidding doors and intruding on some scene of virtuous domesticity. "Contaminate" was the word Hugh's horrid sister had used. She lingered by the furthest window, staring out at the lake, gray and bleak now the sun was off it.

Presently she heard footsteps behind her, and an odiously patronizing voice said, "If it isn't the divine Rosalba! So you've come to visit me at last."

As he was, strictly speaking, her host, she could hardly tell Gus Rainham to go away, so she merely said, "I did not know you would be here, Sir Augustus, and I shall be leaving very soon."

"Driven off by those squawking hens, eh? You need not be. I am the master here, and if I order my wife to receive any little friend of mine, it is her duty to obey me."

Rosalba eyed him contemptuously and with an irrational sense of outrage on Lady Alicia's behalf. Was he really capable of humiliating his wife in her own house, or was it just a piece of bravado? He was such a mixture of depravity and silliness it was hard to tell.

Lolling against a marble console table which stood between the windows, he looked rather less unhealthy than she remembered him. Early hours and country air must have done him good against his will. Even so, his loose, leering mouth and his thick white hands were repulsive, and he smelled of stale sweat. If he tries to touch me, she thought, I shall be sick.

"So you deserted that husband of yours for my self-righteous cousin," he was saying. "I knew you weren't as prim as you pretended."

"That is not at all what happened!"

"I'm not blaming you, though you'd have done better to come to me; I'm three times as rich as Hugh. But you're well rid of Carlow. I wonder how he's getting on among the frogs."

"Among the frogs?" she repeated, puzzled by this strange expression. "What do you mean?"

"He's gone to Paris, didn't you know? That rackety fellow Dan Robinson went with him. They mean to make their fortune over there, and good luck to them, I say. I hate the poxy French."

Rosalba was so intrigued by this news that she almost forgot her dislike of Gus, and would have asked for more details, if Hugh had not appeared, looking as black as thunder.

"What the devil are you doing here?" he asked his cousin, somewhat unreasonably.

"Damn it all, I live here. This is my house." Gus added with a malicious grin, "I've been entertaining Mrs. Carlow."

"Mrs. York," said Hugh shortly. "I hope he has done nothing to displease you, Rosalba."

"Of course not." She thought Hugh was being rather high-handed. "If you have finished talking to your relations, I should like to start for London at once."

"Shall we not have our picnic first? You'd like some hot soup to warm you before the journey."

"I don't want any soup. I simply want to leave this house."

"Very well," said Hugh, seeing this was no time to argue. Once they were in the carriage, he began to apologize.

"I am sorry my sister was so rude to you. Don't take it too hard. She is ill-informed on some points, like many respectable women, and I think she was particularly chagrined to discover that you were a lady, someone they actually mistook for a very well-connected acquaintance of my cousin William."

"You said there would be no one there."

"Gus and Alicia were supposed to be remaining in Hampshire until after her confinement. But he is quite unpredictable."

"In that case you should have taken the trouble to find out whether they were at Liston."

Rosalba was now furious with Hugh, blaming him for the discomforts of the last hour.

"Yes, I know I should, and I'm truly sorry, my little love," he said peaceably. "Such a thing will never happen again."

"It most certainly will not, for I shall never trust you to take me anywhere. I can understand why Margaret is so retiring. I suppose Roche is as selfish and thoughtless as you are."

Hugh did not attempt to defend himself, and for the next ten minutes they drove in silence.

Then he said, "Do you think you might feel better if you had something to eat?"

"I'm not hungry."

"I am. Would it disturb you if I opened the hamper?"

"Not in the least. I suppose you are incapable of curbing your brutish appetites," said Rosalba coldly.

His mouth screwed up as though he was trying not to laugh. And if he does, she decided, I'll hit him. However, he remained commendably grave. He opened the basket, spread a white napkin on his knee, and started to investigate the delicacies that Rosalba's cook had packed for them.

Rosalba felt extremely ill-used. She realized too late that in fact she was ravenously hungry, and the scent of fresh bread, rich pastry, spiced brawn and apples tormented her like an actual shaft of pain in her stomach. She gazed resolutely out of the carriage window at the dull winter commons of Middlesex, but was drawn unwillingly back to the man beside her. Their eyes met.

"Are you still angry with me?" he inquired.

"You don't care if I am."

"Not very much." He flicked a crumb off his coat sleeve. "Would you like to know why?"

She bit her lip to stop it trembling.

"When I first took you to Hunsden Street," said Hugh, "you approved of everything so readily, you were so compliant to all my wishes, I could hardly get you to express a divergent opinion. I was a little surprised. It is very pleasant to be agreed with, but not all the time, and besides, I was sure you had a mind of your own. Then it dawned on me that you felt obliged to agree with everything I suggested, out of gratitude, and perhaps from the fear of antagonizing me. Because we are not married, you have found it hard to believe that you have any hold over me. Though lately I am glad to say you have begun to spar with me, and today you are as cross as any lawful wedded wife. Dear Rosalba, you can't think what a relief that is."

She was struck dumb by this unexpected view of herself. Yet there was some sense in it. She would not have dared to be so disagreeable, tried to make him lose his maddening composure or his temper, if she had been afraid of losing his love.

"You wretch," she said. "You have no right to be so confoundedly clever. And sitting there eating your head off, when you know I am positively starving."

Smiling, Hugh handed her a chicken leg out of the hamper. All grievances were forgotten; she was immensely, blindingly happy.

8

Rosalba gave her first card party successfully and began to go about a good deal. There were, after all, plenty of men and women in London who were willing to accept her: not merely lovers paired like herself and Hugh, but artists of every kind, people on the way up, and those whose own lives had, for one reason or another, made them unusually tolerant. She could be seen in public, provided she kept one essential rule; a woman of pleasure must not appear to recognize a man friend when he was in the company of ladies belonging to that other world of society and reputation. But as Rosalba would not go to fashionable places without Hugh, she was never forced to cut him or to see him ignore her. It was the highborn ladies who were sometimes obliged not to notice Hugh.

The only member of the Rainham family she met was Gus. His wife had been safely delivered of a son, a small but healthy child, so the baronet decided he had done his duty and deserved some fun. He no longer tried to make up to Rosalba (much too frightened of his cousin, she thought), though he always seemed pleased to see her and even called in Hunsden Street. Rosalba did not find him a stimulating visitor, and rather hoped Hugh might object.

Hugh merely said that he hoped she might be a good influence on Gus. "And when he is with you, at least I know he is not getting into trouble elsewhere."

One evening when the two Rainhams were drinking tea in Rosalba's drawing room, Hugh said, "I wanted a word with you, Gus. I had a letter this morning from Mr. Sturdy."

"What's he want?"

"He had a somewhat strange suggestion." For some reason Hugh seemed to be feeling his way. He waited while Rosalba refilled his tea bowl.

"Sturdy has got the idea in his head that he might become your tenant at Ashwin. He'd take the place on a repairing lease and move in there for as long as it suited you."

"Rent Ashwin! Why should he?" demanded Gus suspiciously. "What's an old bachelor want with that great barn? Did you put him up to it?"

"Of course not. I agree, the house is far too large for him, but you must remember he is a very keen antiquarian, and I believe the prospect of living and moving about in those ancient rooms may give him a pleasure that not everyone can share. He is a rich man and he can afford to indulge his whims. It might suit you to close with his offer."

"I'll think it over," said Gus grandly.

Rosalba had listened in silence. She waited till Gus had gone before asking, "Who is Mr. Sturdy?"

"A neighbor of ours in Derbyshire, a magistrate and a distinguished scholar. His real reason for wanting to rent Ashwin is that he wishes to look after the house and prevent its becoming a total ruin, but one cannot say so to that stupid little ninny. He is quite irrational about Ashwin. Both my uncle and I have offered to rent the place and be responsible for the upkeep, but he won't listen. Perhaps an outsider like Sturdy may have better luck."

Perhaps he might, for Gus's dog-in-the-manger attitude to the Rainhams' ancestral home was probably connected with his perfectly well-founded suspicion that they all thought him unfit to be the head of the family. He was damned if he'd let them usurp his position, even if they offered to pay for the privilege of living in a house he disliked. Rosalba realized by now how much Hugh minded the neglected state of Ashwin. He felt it so much that he had not been near his native Derbyshire for the last two years. She was sorry for him but could not help remembering that this was somewhere he would never take her.

The season for long journeys into the country had not yet come, but Lord Retford had a villa on the Thames within easy reach of London, and in June Hugh and Rosalba were invited there to join a small, congenial party. Retford and Priscilla Denny were the leaders of their set; he had a mad wife shut away in the country, and after several years of loneliness he had taken Priscilla out of a milliner's shop, educated her to be a companion to him, and placed her in a position superior to most kept mistresses, for she often acted as his hostess in houses which would normally have been the province of his wife. Hugh and Rosalba went by river, gliding lazily on shining water through a green landscape, and when they stepped out of the boat and saw Riverside House, glowing and harmonious like a small palace against a grove of dark trees, Rosalba gave a gasp of pleased astonishment.

The villa had been copied for the present Lord Retford's father from one built in Italy during the Renaissance. It was all on one story (apart from the concealed kitchen and servants' quarters in the basement) and the chief apartment was a fine circular room beneath a high glass dome; this rotunda, as it was called, was enclosed within a square formed by four galleries, each with doorways and ceilings wonderfully gilded and painted in brilliant colors. Hung on the walls was a priceless collection of pictures. There were only four bedrooms, one at each corner of the house. Tonight they would be occupied by four pairs of accredited lovers: Retford and Priscilla Denny, Hugh and Rosalba, St. John Roche and Margaret Lodney, a man called Frederick Hanley and Polly Palmer, the actress. It's like a temple of love, thought Rosalba, when they had been shown round.

They spent a very pleasant day pretending to fish (only the sun was too bright), inspecting the botanical rarities in the greenhouse, conversing in the shade. When she had first got to know Hugh and his friends, Rosalba had been intimidated by their clever talk; she had sat in silence, an ignorant provincial. Now she had learned to join in; Hugh had educated her, given her books to read, and she had developed the gift of exchanging ideas, of catching an allusion or turning an argument with a sudden shaft of wit. All the women, like their men, understood the art of conversation. In this particular set it was not enough simply to be beautiful and amorous.

Today the only person who did not contribute was Margaret, and this was certainly not due to stupidity. She sat gazing over the river, wan and withdrawn, answering in a low voice when spoken to directly and then falling silent.

"What do you think is wrong with her?" Rosalba asked Hugh when they went to dress for dinner.

"The same thing that has been wrong with her ever since she and Roche ran off together. The fear that she will not be able to keep him beside her forever."

Poor Margaret.

They dined in the rotunda at a circular table under the glass dome with a wind band playing in a concealed gallery. After dinner Fred Hanley, who was a keen astronomer, produced a telescope, which he wanted to set up on the terrace in order to study the night sky. It was still too light for any stars to show, but Hanley became engrossed in showing off the finer points of his telescope to Hugh, who was always fascinated by scientific instruments. They began to talk about the transit of Venus which they had both been able to observe last year.

Retford suggested that some of the party might care for another stroll in the garden now the heat had gone out of the day. He set off down the steps with Rosalba, Polly and St.

John Roche. Margaret seemed about to get up and follow them, then she changed her mind, evidently determined not to pursue her lover wherever he went. All the other couples had temporarily separated, in accordance with civilized social custom.

It was pleasant in the dusky alleys with the evening scent of herbs and crushed grass under their feet. At first they moved along together in a quartet, but gradually Rosalba found that she and Roche were falling behind as he began to talk about Margaret.

"God knows, I don't mean to complain, after all she has given up for my sake. Only she cannot bear to have me out of her sight. I do find her attitude unreasonable."

"But you are out of her sight quite often," Rosalba pointed out. "I am forever meeting you shopping in Bond Street or driving in the park. Or at a play."

"Well, there you are! Margaret insists that she cannot accompany me to such places, yet you go happily enough with Rainham. And your situation is not so very different."

Rosalba had no intention of comparing their exact degrees of immorality and guilt. She never let her mind run on this subject, and in the present setting it would be thoroughly out of place.

Instead she said, "Margaret shrinks from going to places where she runs the risk of being cold-shouldered by her old friends. I am in no such danger. I had no respectable acquaintances in London when I met Hugh."

"Hugh is a lucky fellow. I envy him."

This was said with such feeling that Rosalba did not know how to answer, so she said nothing.

"How charming you look in your green-and-white dress," he persisted. "Like a flower. Fair rose of May. Doesn't that come out of Shakespeare?"

"It is Laertes' description of his sister Ophelia, after she has gone mad. So I do not consider it appropriate," said Rosalba repressively.

"By no means! My feelings for you are anything but brotherly," said St. John Roche, insinuating an arm round her shoulders, so that his hand came out with fingers spread, to

73

press hard against the softness of her breast.

He began to kiss her face and neck.

"How dare you, sir! Let me go at once!" exclaimed Rosalba.

He did loosen his hold for a moment, but only to say, in a practical manner, "Shall we go into that pavilion over there? I fancy there is some sort of daybed we can lie on, and we may never get a better opportunity."

Rosalba gaped at him. "One of us has certainly gone mad. Are you suggesting that I might let you make love to me?"

"Why not? It seems the most natural request—"

"Why not? Don't Hugh and Margaret provide sufficient reasons?"

"Oh, for heaven's sake—what has it got to do with them? We are not married to them. You've played this game too often to waste time on fine sentiments. Or are you afraid of being caught? That usually adds an extra spice."

Rosalba was shocked. Here was Margaret's devoted lover, inviting her into a garden pavilion for a furtive erotic tumble, hinting that the danger of discovery might add an extra excitement—and worst of all, he was apparently convinced that she was used to such degrading adventures. Was it possible that women like herself were expected to behave in such a way at scandalous houseparties where all the unions were illicit? This seemed too outrageous. (Distantly through the trees she could hear Retford and Polly chatting amiably; they did not sound in the least impassioned.) As Roche reached out for Rosalba's hand, she turned and ran.

Racing across the grass, her skirt rippling behind her like the crest of a wave, she told herself she must not lose her head. If she appeared like this in front of the terrace, there would be awkward questions to answer. She chose an inferior flight of stairs at the back of the house and climbed them in stumbling haste. She thought Roche was following her. She would take refuge in her own room. Running along the gallery, she turned left and at last flung herself into the bedroom with all the triumph and relief of a child playing hide-and-seek.

It was too dark to make out anything in there beyond the vague shape of the canopy over the bed and the shimmer of the dressing-table mirror. Rosalba stood gasping to get her breath. She thought she was safe, when to her utter astonishment Roche came in after her, his masculine impudence quite unimpaired.

"So this is where you fled to. I guessed you might."

"Get out of my room this instant!"

"But it isn't your room, is it, my sweet hypocrite? It's mine."

For the first time Rosalba took in the brushes and bottles and items of clothing, none of which belonged to her and Hugh. Coming into the villa from the wrong side and in a stupid panic, she had lost her sense of direction and made for the room occupied by Roche and Margaret.

And of course this conceited libertine refused to believe she had done it by mistake. He made a grab for her; she kicked him on the instep, which only seemed to stimulate his enthusiasm.

"So you enjoy a sham battle? Some women do—when they are sure of losing."

Then they both heard an intrusive sound in the apparently empty house: feminine heels clicking on the floor outside. Roche's intentions changed in a flash.

"That's Margaret—she mustn't find you here!"

With hands that were far from caressing he steered Rosalba towards a closet at the back of the room, thrust her inside and closed the door on her.

Rosalba found herself in total darkness. Almost holding her breath, she heard Roche and Margaret talking in the room outside.

"Why were you away so long?" she was asking him. "I thought you'd never come back. I decided to come and look for you in the garden—I came to fetch a shawl—"

"My dear Meg, you really must learn to control your feelings. I wish you would stop chasing after me like a hen with one chick. You are making us both ridiculous—surely you can see it?"

"Oh, please don't scold me. I know how foolish I must seem to you, yet I cannot help seeing how all those other women look at you, hoping to take you away from me if they can."

Well, here's one who has no desire to compete, thought

Rosalba. And what a stupid thing to tell him, making him more conceited than he is already. Hasn't she any pride?

It sounded now as though Margaret was crying and Roche—the snake—comforting her with lies about his eternal fidelity. Perhaps he was going to make love to her while Rosalba was forced to stay in this black hole and listen. Perhaps Margaret would settle down for the night, and Rosalba would be unable to escape. Presently she would be missed, there would be a search; it was all too like an absurd farce, only the resulting scene would not be at all amusing. Margaret would be distraught, and Hugh—Rosalba had no idea how Hugh would respond. Would he ever believe that she had gone into the wrong room by accident? It did sound an incredibly lame explanation, and how far would she feel able to trust a woman whom he himself had seduced so easily?

She was thinking these gloomy thoughts when she realized that the kissing and crying had stopped, and the couple were preparing to leave the bedroom, Roche saying in a loud, cheerful voice that it would be cool on the terrace and Meg would certainly need her shawl.

Rosalba heard them go with a great surge of thankfulness. She waited a few minutes, hearing nothing beyond the drum of her own heartbeats, and then crept out of the closet and across the bedroom and into the gallery, which was now filled with a glow of warm light from the wall sconces. She paused to enjoy the sensation of freedom.

"You're quite safe now," said a man's voice a few feet away from her.

Rosalba jumped.

Standing against the opposite wall, in front of a huge painting of his ancestors by Van Dyck, Lord Retford was watching her.

"How—how you made me jump, my lord," gulped Rosalba. "I was—looking for Margaret."

"No, really. That won't do," said her host, apparently amused.

She gazed at him in alarm. She had never known quite what to make of this smooth-tongued nobleman. She supposed he had jumped to the obvious conclusion, but was he simply

76

mocking her or was there something else behind the mockery? He and Hugh were very close friends.

"I may as well tell you," he said, "that while we were in the garden I caught sight of you running across the lawn. You have an excellent turn of speed. I found it a more interesting transit of Venus than anything those two astronomers are likely to see through their telescopes."

"Then you must have seen that I was running away from Mr. Roche. Not into his arms."

"Yes, I did. So when I got back to the house and found no sign of either of you, I thought I might investigate. What I don't perfectly understand—"

"I know," interrupted Rosalba. "You can't think why I was in that room, and it is too mortifying, because you are never going to believe me when I tell you."

The odd thing was that he did believe her immediately. He had known the house since his childhood and agreed at once that the four galleries were extremely confusing; strangers were constantly getting lost.

"One comes to treat the paintings as landmarks," he said. "You could hardly be expected to do that."

Finding she had nothing to fear from Retford, Rosalba told him exactly what she thought of Roche.

"And if his behavior to Margaret is not bad enough," she concluded, "I don't see what reason he has to come pestering me. I swear I never encouraged him."

"He has probably heard misleading reports of your character."

"From who?" she asked ungrammatically.

"From Gus Rainham."

"Oh?" Rosalba flushed. "I thought Hugh's friends already knew the story of my marriage and how we first met. I assumed that he had told you."

"Yes, but the lamentable Gus has chosen to rearrange the facts a little. He has put it about that you and your husband were very well suited until you left him for Hugh. That until then he had been living on your earnings."

Rosalba was speechless. She stared at Retford, too angry and disgusted even to protest.

At last she whispered, "Do people believe that?"

"Certainly not. No one who matters pays any attention to Gus. If Roche is the exception, I am afraid that is because he wants to make love to you and would like to believe you are as promiscuous as he is."

"Well, I hope you are right. Why should Gus say anything so horrible? I thought he liked me. I have often tried to take his part when I thought Hugh was being a little hard on him."

"He's a vindictive little viper," remarked Retford. "And he's always been jealous of Hugh. How much do you propose to tell Hugh of all this?"

She was uncertain. "I've never concealed anything from him before."

"If you take my advice, you'll keep quiet about your encounter with Roche. If Hugh finds out, there'll be a regular fireworks display. Have you ever seen him in one of his rages? He has a very violent temper, for all he's such a cool customer in the ordinary way. And though I agree that Roche deserves no quarter, if those two were to quarrel, you know who would be the chief sufferer."

"Margaret," said Rosalba unhappily. "No, I don't want that to happen. I don't want to make trouble. All the same, I don't feel inclined to let Gus go on slandering me. If a man tells the same lie often enough, someone is bound to believe him in the end."

"Leave it to me," said Retford. "I'll let Hugh know what Gus has been up to, without any reference to yourself and Roche. Try to assume an air of composure, my dear, for I can hear our stargazers coming in from the terrace."

When the rest of the party entered the gallery he was holding up a branched candlestick so that Rosalba could examine the masterly brushstrokes of his favorite Raphael.

In bed that night, Hugh said, "You had a long tête-à-tête with Retford. Was he trying to make love to you?"

"Of course not!" she exclaimed in honest surprise, for among all the dangerous possibilities of the evening, that one had not crossed her mind.

"Good," said Hugh, apparently satisfied.

"Surely you did not suspect him—or me either, I hope?"

"No," he admitted, stroking back her hair with his fingers,

so that he could kiss the line just where it grew away from her forehead. "But he is very successful with women, and there is no sense in taking too much for granted."

One of the shutters was half open and a transparent radiance of moonlight seeped into the room, so that she felt as though they could see in the dark.

"What would you do," she whispered, "if you caught one of your friends making love to me?"

"Kill him," said Hugh promptly. "And then, my siren, I should carry you off to a moated grange in the depths of the country, and keep you under lock and key for the rest of your life."

9

Roche and Margaret left Waterside House next day. Margaret was reputed to be starting one of her headaches and must go home at once to recover in darkened silence.

"She thinks herself too good to mix with courtesans and actresses," said Priscilla calmly. "Though I don't believe any of us has yet deserted a child in its cradle."

Rosalba did not try to defend Margaret, though she thought privately that this time it was probably Roche who had wanted to leave in a hurry, to avoid the awkwardness of being in her company and the fear that she might complain to Hugh about him.

The rest of their visit passed very enjoyably. Rosalba kept wondering when Retford was going to speak to Hugh about Gus, but it was not until their last evening that the two men sat up talking very late—so late that she was asleep when Hugh came to bed and he did not wake her.

They traveled home by river as far as Westminster Stairs, where Hugh had arranged for his carriage to meet them. He instructed his coachman to drive first to Grosvenor Street and put him down, before conveying Mrs. York to her own house.

"Are you going to call on Gus?" asked Rosalba, all innocent curiosity.

"Yes."

Nothing more. The cool customer, she thought, glancing sideways at him and recalling Retford's words. Could he really lose his temper so dramatically? She had never seen him do so; he usually managed to get what he wanted without raising his voice.

When they reached Grosvenor Street and stopped outside Sir Augustus Rainham's impressive town house, Hugh lifted her hand to his lips in a gentle farewell.

"We must part for the present, dear heart. I'm engaged this evening, as I told you, but I'll dine with you tomorrow."

It only now dawned on Rosalba that she would have to wait twenty-four hours before finding out the result of his visit to Gus. This did not suit her at all, so as she saw Hugh being admitted to the house, she called out to the coachman that they would wait here for Mr. Rainham after all. She was rather a favorite with the coachman, who knew he would not get into trouble with his master for obeying an order of hers, so he made no objection.

Rosalba was leaning out of the carriage, surveying the passersby, when she caught sight of a man who seemed somehow familiar. He was fairly young, not very tall and quietly dressed; not at all showy, but he had a good figure and a good tailor. She was wondering idly where she had seen him before, and their eyes met. He stopped and took off his hat.

"Good Morning, Mrs. Carlow."

The hated name gave her a jolt. This must be someone she had met during the uneasy months of her marriage, but who? He looked too respectable to be one of Carlow's gaming cronies, too polished for one of their dupes.

"You don't remember me," he said with a diffident smile. "John Meade. Your husband brought you to my chambers shortly after you were married."

He was the young attorney who had looked at her with such compassion when Carlow made it painfully clear that he had married her simply to fulfill the terms of his grandmother's bequest—and that he felt he had made a bad bargain. Instead of the heavy, old-fashioned wig of the legal profession Mr. Meade was today wearing a tye-wig, the hair unpowdered and drawn back in a queue.

"Of course I recognize you," she said.

"I had heard you were in France. The climate must have suited you, for there is no need to inquire after your health."

What John Meade would have heard was that Carlow was in France. Obviously he did not know they had separated; the sight of Rosalba's glowing looks as she sat in a private carriage in this aristocratic street must have suggested that the Edgar Carlows were unexpectedly prosperous.

Just as she was wondering whether she ought to correct this false impression, the matter explained itself, for Hugh came out of his cousin's house and down the steps in two brisk strides. He was moving so fast that Mr. Meade automatically stepped back. Hugh, simply seeing a man on the pavement, did not realize that this person had anything to do with Rosalba, and he spoke to her without any conventional formality.

"I didn't intend you to wait for me, my love. However, it's just as well you did, for Gus can't be found. The servants say he must have gone out without telling them. So I can come home with you after all."

As he stepped into the carriage, Rosalba saw over his shoulder Mr. Meade's face grow pink, either from disapproval or sheer embarrassment. Hugh's confidently affectionate manner made their relationship clearer than any number of languishing glances would have done. The lawyer made her a very slight bow and walked off.

Hugh was now telling the coachman he could take them to Hunsden Street, though at the moment it was impossible for him to take them anywhere; some way in front of them a hackney carriage going towards Bond Street had almost collided with a private chaise coming towards Grosvenor Square, and everyone was held up while their cursing drivers tried to proceed, gingerly scraping each other's paint. Hugh and Rosalba sat waiting, and she was beginning to tell him about Mr. Meade when the door of Sir Augustus Rainham's house opened again, and the owner himself sidled out.

"Good gracious," said Rosalba. "He was in there all the time."

Hugh flung back the door of the carriage and jumped down on to the pavement.

Gus had taken such care to look left and right before descending the steps that he had not noticed his cousin's carriage held up immediately in front of him. Hugh's sudden appearance gave him a nasty fright.

"What do you want?" he asked ungraciously.

"To see you, my dear Augustus. Why did you make them tell me you'd gone out?"

"I—I have an engagement. A fellow is not obliged to be at home to everyone who calls, and if you simply came because you heard I had a spell of bad luck at Selby's the other night—"

"I should not care if you lost every shilling you possess. I've done with trying to keep you out of trouble. But I won't have you telling scurrilous stories about a woman you once tried to injure and who generously forgave you. Do you understand me, you little viper?"

"I don't know what you're talking about!" blustered Gus, but the words ended on a squeak of apprehension, and his glance flew guiltily towards Rosalba in the carriage.

"There's no point in denying what you said, for Retford heard it all."

With Hugh towering over him like a grim figure of Nemesis, Gus had to rack his wits for some kind of excuse.

"I fear Retford mistook my meaning. It was a jest, no more. I may have suggested that I once made use of Rosalba's bed—something of that kind—it was true in a sense, you know."

Hugh knocked him down.

Gus fell in a sprawling position and lay moaning on the flagstones.

"Get up," said Hugh in a cold, furious voice. "And don't let me ever again hear of you taking away her character, or I'll break your neck."

Gus clambered to his feet. His hat and wig had fallen off and his nose was bleeding.

"She hasn't any character to take away," he muttered thickly.

"No, Hugh—don't!" cried Rosalba, seeing that Hugh was about to hit him a second time.

She too jumped down from the carriage and caught her lover's arm. A crowd was beginning to collect. It was true that the quarreling coachmen further along the street were making enough commotion to mask a scene so unusual in this sedate region of Mayfair; even so, a party of fashionably dressed ladies had paused in horror, two chairmen were frankly gaping, and a portly clergyman took Hugh to task.

"I must ask you, sir, to desist from such ungentlemanly brawling in a public street. You should be ashamed of attacking this unfortunate young man, who is much smaller than yourself and not at all strong by the look of him."

Hugh said through his teeth, "This is a family matter, sir. Be so good as to mind your own business."

The clergyman gobbled like a turkey cock.

"Do leave Gus alone, Hugh," begged Rosalba. "And get back into the carriage. Look, the traffic is moving, and it is we who are blocking the road now."

Hugh gave in reluctantly. Through the sleeve of his coat she could feel him trembling with rage. Gus was leaning against the area railings, mopping his bloody nose. He shouted after Hugh in an excess of hatred that yet managed to extract a feeble triumph.

"Very well, you hulking bully—I'll pay you out. Your friend Sturdy can whistle for his lease. I'll sell the lead off the roof and leave the house to fall down, and you won't be able to stop me!"

Rosalba was thankful that the carriage was able to move on. She felt impelled to ask Hugh exactly what Gus had said about her. Of course she knew already but felt it would seem odd if she remained incurious.

"He made some poisonous allegations that I don't need to repeat. After this you will never be obliged to speak to him again."

He refused to talk about what had happened, or about anything else, and though he returned to Hunsden Street with her, he went on looking like a thundercloud for the rest of the afternoon. It was very exhausting.

At last Rosalba decided to go into the attack.

"I have a pretty shrewd idea what sort of stories Gus would have made up about me—I'd be a fool if I couldn't guess. So why are you so unreasonably angry? You've punished him now and put a stop to his malice, so why go on brooding over them?"

He was standing by the drawing-room window, hands in pockets, gazing absently at a pink geranium in a china pot, placed there to catch the sun. His expression, sullen and remote, made her think fancifully of how a volcano might look after the flames had subsided.

He said, "It's not really Gus I'm angry with now—I've done with him. I am the one who is to blame. I should never have tempted you into a position where any scoundrel can make up vile accusations about you."

"Nonsense," said Rosalba, taking his hand and lifting up her face to be kissed. "Carlow placed me in that position, and your presence has protected me ever since from hearing what they choose to say."

If this was not wholly true, if his presence had actually made a false accusation valid, she did not want to dwell on these fine points of morality, so she changed the subject.

"What do you suppose Gus meant about letting a house fall down? Which house?"

"Ashwin. He means to refuse Sturdy's offer."

She remembered now. "Mr. Sturdy is your antiquarian friend in Derbyshire who wants to rent Ashwin because he has a passion for old houses. Don't you think Gus was just being spiteful? That he may change his mind?"

"Not he," said Hugh bitterly. "It's hard on poor Sturdy. I lost my temper, so Gus will take care that nothing is done at Ashwin that might give me pleasure. Petty malice is the one incentive that can inspire him to persevere in any course of action."

They were sitting on the sofa by now. Hugh had his arm round Rosalba and her head was on his shoulder. He sounded disconsolate.

"I had thought of going to Derbyshire on my way back from Yorkshire in the autumn, if Sturdy was in possession by then."

Rosalba knew that Hugh's mother had belonged to a great Yorkshire family, and that he went up there every year to see his maternal relations and to enjoy some shooting and fishing. Naturally he could not take her with him. He loved her, he became fierce in her defense, he felt a deep remorse because he knew he had made her vulnerable to insult—yet he took it for granted that they should separate for several months in the summer and autumn when men of his standing all went out of town. She did not comment.

With so much on her mind, she hardly thought about her brief meeting with Mr. John Meade. In any case she never expected to see him again and was taken by surprise, three days later, when he called on her in Hunsden Street.

"I hope you don't object to receiving me, ma'am," he began, as soon as the servant had shown him into the drawing room, where Rosalba was sitting alone; she had just dined, but it was still rather early for most people to pay visits.

"I am delighted to see you," she said hastily, hoping her expression had not seemed unwelcoming. "Do pray be seated. I was wondering how you were able to find me."

"It was not very difficult."

No, she thought, it wouldn't have been. That was a stupid question. Hugh was fairly well known; a man like Meade would probably have recognized him. It would have been simple to find out through coffee-house gossip where the wealthy Mr. Rainham kept his current mistress.

"I understand you are using your maiden name," said the lawyer. "I believe—that is to say, I am simply guessing, for I have no firsthand information—I assume that you felt obliged to leave Carlow because he ill-treated you or made your life intolerable. It does not surprise me."

"I did not leave him, as it happens. He left me. He did his best to drag me into a criminal conspiracy, and when that failed, he robbed me of my few small possessions and crept out of our lodging, leaving me with seven shillings in the world and weeks of unpaid rent. If Mr. Rainham had not come to my rescue, I should be languishing in a debtors' prison at this moment."

"Surely you need not have accepted help from such a quarter! Why did you not apply to us, ma'am? You are a member of the Carlow family, and I feel certain your brother-in-law would have been ready to assist you in such a desperate case."

"I did apply to you," retorted Rosalba with some asperity.

85

"I sent a note round to Lincoln's Inn and received an immediate reply that you yourself were not available and that his family had repudiated all further responsibility for my husband's actions."

"Great heavens, this is horrible!" Mr. Meade sounded quite overcome. "I can guess who was to blame—our chief clerk, a presumptuous jack-in-office who always supposes he knows how to settle everything. He never even told me of your plight. I'll skin him alive when I get back to chambers. Not that this is of much consequence to you now. I can only say how sorry I am that we failed you so disastrously."

"Well, I can see now that it was not your fault. And I am not in a sponging house, so there is nothing to distress you."

Meade did not seem to be attending. He said, "It is quite atrocious that you should have been forced into your present unhappy situation—"

"My present *what?*"

"All this," said the lawyer, taking a comprehensive glance round the pretty, luxurious drawing room and including in his inventory the harpsichord and the games table. "This house and everything in it paid for, I suppose by—I don't wish to offend you, ma'am, but this is not the sort of life you were brought up to."

"If you don't wish to offend me, you would be wise to stop making veiled attacks on Mr. Rainham. Do you suppose he paid my debts so that I should be compelled to take him as my lover? Then let me tell you, sir, you are quite mistaken. At the time he settled my arrears of rent, he gave me the money for my coach fare back to Suffolk. When he discovered that I had stayed in London he did his best to find me some respectable employment. It was only then that he discovered our mutual liking had grown into an attachment which—in other words, we fell in love, and whatever you think of my conduct, Mr. Meade, I don't see that you have any reason to come here and preach at me."

Mr. Meade seemed to have been totally vanquished by this speech. "I should not dream of passing any sort of judgment," he assured her, and added, "How splendid you look when you are angry."

This unstudied compliment melted her annoyance. For the

remainder of his visit they spoke of general subjects, and she found him sympathetic and well informed. When he rose to go, he asked if he might call again. Rosalba agreed. She felt she had made an agreeable new friend.

10

The delights of June in London—the beauty of the river and the parks, starlit evenings at Vauxhall or Ranelagh—were overshadowed for Rosalba by the knowledge that she and Hugh would soon be parted, perhaps for as long as four months. The idea made her miserable. Their separation at Christmas had been quite different, for besides being very short, she had not then minded being alone. After the uncomfortable kind of loneliness of living with people she did not care for, she had found a certain charm in living so comfortably by herself. Now she had been spoiled. The house in Hunsden Street meant nothing if Hugh was not there.

And just when her spirits were sinking, she had an additional shock. She realized that she was pregnant. She could hardly believe her bad luck. After living five months with Carlow and nearly eight with Hugh, she had come to feel herself immune from the common fate of women. She did not want a child. Her youthful dreams of bringing up a family had been crushed down as soon as she realized what sort of a man she had married and the wandering, precarious life they were going to lead. She had never allowed those hopes to revive. The birth of a baby would be the most tiresome interruption to her present way of life, and what was to become of the poor little unwanted creature? Hugh would hardly welcome a bastard child; still less would he want a reunion, several months from now, with a mistress grown repulsive and lethargic, quite unfit for the lively amusements of winter and the pleasures of love. I might lose him altogether, she thought. My hold on him is very likely to weaken while he is away from me, and if he comes back and finds me dull and ugly, it will never be the same again. He would provide for her and the child, but what did she care about that? She could not bring herself to tell him or anyone else what had happened, feeling that as long as she kept quiet, the baby would not become a real fact. Perhaps she would have a miscarriage.

"Are you feeling quite well, my love?" Hugh asked her. "You look very pale."

"It's the effect of wearing powder. I know it doesn't suit me."

They were dining in Hunsden Street, both very finely dressed, for they were going to a musical party that Priscilla was giving and that was to be as elegant as any in the most elevated circles this season. Hugh wore a royal blue coat and a flower-embroidered waistcoat, the queue of his white wig neatly secured in a black satin bag; Rosalba's pink-and-silver dress was new and very becoming, and she had spent some hours having her hair curled, pomaded and powdered by an artist of genius, though it was true that the strange fashion for white or gray hair did not really improve her, the contrast between her dark locks and clear, delicate skin being one of her chief assets.

"You haven't eaten much," persisted Hugh.

They had nearly finished their meal; the dishes and tureens stood on the table around them, and there still seemed to be a great deal of delicious food left: poached salmon, roast duckling, green peas, strawberry tarts. He saw Rosalba lay down her fork.

"You've lost your appetite."

"It's been a hot day."

"You need some good fresh air. In fact, I've been making arrangements for you to spend the summer in a very pretty part of the country."

He paused, having decided to cut himself a piece of cheese. Rosalba felt her heart thumping. She thought, He's taking me to Yorkshire after all. He would put her in a discreet lodging not too far from his relations, where he could visit her.

Hugh said, "Roche has taken a house for Margaret near Sevenoaks, and you are to share it with them."

"No!"

Hugh was rather startled by her vehemence. He looked

88

at her in surprise, and said, "I thought you would be pleased. What is your objection?"

She had never told him of Roche's attempt to make love to her while they were at Retford's villa. She had followed Retford's advice; having seen Hugh deal with Gus, she knew she had been wise. If he knew the truth there would have been a violent quarrel, perhaps even a duel.

"You must have some reason," he pressed her.

"Well, I don't wish to sound unkind, but poor Margaret is not a very cheerful companion. If we are to be shut up in some rural paradise—"

"If it was just the two of you, I agree that Margaret might become rather doleful. But St. John will be there too, you know. He means to spend most of July and August in Kent."

He would, she thought. What a traitor the man is, both to his love and his friend. It was probably he who had suggested the whole plan to Hugh. Although Rosalba had gloomy visions of herself growing heavy and shapeless later on, she knew that she had still some months of graceful activity ahead of her, and she did not wish to spend them running away from St. John Roche in the confined space of a small rented cottage and trying to prevent Margaret from noticing what was going on.

So she said, "I don't want to go to Kent."

"A pity I wasted my time," said Hugh stiffly. He sounded hurt because his well-meaning efforts had not been appreciated. "Where do you want to go?"

There was no point in saying Yorkshire (that was the kind of silly mistake Margaret would have made). More or less at random, Rosalba suggested, "I might go to Ireland with Kitty Kerrigan."

Mrs. Kerrigan was a beguiling widow who had made herself so amenable during the past ten years that she was now able to live more or less as she pleased.

"You must be mad!" exclaimed Hugh. "You don't imagine I'd allow you to go running about Dublin with that trollop."

There were several things about this pronouncement that annoyed Rosalba, and she said crossly, "I don't know why you should make any distinction. If she's a trollop, so am I."

"Of course you know the difference. The Kerrigan is a rapacious bloodsucker. She's had a string of men—"

"What of it? I can't see that it matters."

She had no real wish to enter Irish society with such a notorious companion, but she felt aggrieved; she had been forced to concoct this unsuitable plan simply to protect Hugh from quarreling with Roche and setting their small circle by the ears. She began to say things she might soon regret.

"One lover or twenty, I'm considered no more fit than Kitty Kerrigan to meet your aristocratic friends. Though why ladies of quality should choose to play the part of shrinking vestals I cannot imagine, for they nearly all have lovers of their own, only they dare not say so, and the whole of the polite world connives in their hypocrisy."

"I'm sorry," said Hugh uncomfortably. "It must seem unjust to you. It *is* unjust. But you knew from the start what the position was going to be. I didn't make the rules."

"No, but they suit you well enough. All you men are the same," she said, hating him for making her pregnant. "You and Carlow and Roche and Gus—you can be as dissolute and heartless as you choose, and go unpunished, while we are your slaves and prisoners, made to suffer for your misdeeds."

Naturally he did not understand what had brought on this outburst, and said tersely, "Do stop talking fustian, Rosalba."

"It's not fustian." Rosalba reached for the brandy decanter, poured some into a glass and drank it off. "You and Carlow, between you, have made me what I am today. I wouldn't have believed, a year ago, that I could come to this. A kept woman, one degree higher than a public harlot."

She was trying to goad him. He was equally determined not to be goaded. He stood up, glancing at the clock.

"The chairs will be here in a minute. Are you ready to start?"

"I'm not coming."

"Don't be childish, Rosalba. There's no sense in sulking."

"Please stop patronizing me. I suppose you think I am obliged to do anything you ask, because I have no money and you are so good as to feed and clothe me—"

"But of course! Haven't we agreed that you are my slave and prisoner, only one degree better than a harlot? And not many degrees better than a fishwife, judging from your conversation. Go and put on your cloak before I drag you screaming into the street."

He was laughing at her. It was the final straw. Men could make him angry, even a man as contemptible as his cousin Gus, but she was only a pet, a chattel; her antagonism merely amused him. Temper, chagrin and brandy pulsed through her veins, and she longed to make him sorry.

Jumping up, she ran from the room. She had thought of a way to pay him out.

Upstairs in the bedroom she paused, surveying herself in the glass. The fashionable but discreet décolletage at the front of her dress was edged with a soft and becoming border of blond lace. Rosalba picked up her scissors, snipped at the stitching and then gave a brisk tug. A stream of silky lace came away in her hand. The top of her dress was now nearly two inches lower, the outward curving lines of her breast were clearly revealed, the nipples just hidden by a provokingly narrow margin of brocade. He won't like that, she thought with satisfaction, dipping the hare's foot into her pot of rouge and laying a bright carmine daub high on each cheekbone. She was accustomed to using paint very delicately, and these hectic splashes of color made her look quite different and much older. Reaching for her patch-glass, she stuck two little black discs at the corner of her mouth for good measure. What else? Foraging in her trinket box, she found and put on a coral brooch and a garnet necklace which clashed with her dress and with each other. As an afterthought, she selected a pompom of orange and yellow artificial flowers and pushed it into the charming ornament of pearls and moonstones carefully placed by the hairdressers.

I do look astoundingly vulgar, she told herself, pleased and amused. Her mischievous impulse might have subsided but for the brandy; although she was certainly not drunk, the effect of the spirit, when she had eaten so little, had made her light-headed and irresponsible.

She could hear Hugh calling her from downstairs. She put on her cloak and carefully arranged the hood to cover her hair and shade her face. Hugh was already out on the pavement, showing signs of impatience, and hardly looked at her as she stepped into her chair. He got into the second chair, the men took up the poles, and they were carried through streets still panting from the heat of the sun which had barely dipped behind the rooftops.

The altercation at dinner had made them late, and when they arrived at Priscilla Denny's house there was no one in the hall apart from two footmen. Though it was still light outside, the curtains had been drawn and the place was ablaze with candles. Rosalba was shown into a side room where the ladies had left their wraps. Already from the floor above she could hear the powerful voice of an Italian opera singer entertaining the company.

Appearing in all her flamboyance, Rosalba found Hugh waiting for her at the foot of the stairs and looking, she had to admit, very striking in his dress coat and powder. He caught the first astonishing impact of the indecently low-cut dress, the painted cheeks, the vulgar profusion of ill-matched ornaments. For an instant he was paralyzed by sheer incredulity. Then he stepped forward and caught her by the arm.

"You little devil, what do you mean by playing me such a trick?"

He had gone quite white with anger—no question now that she could make him lose his temper. The grip of his hand was hard and painful.

"You're hurting me!" she protested.

He said in a low voice, "If you choose to behave like a strumpet you must expect to be treated like a strumpet. But you won't make a public exhibition of yourself. I'm going to take you straight home and give you a lesson in decorum."

He turned her sharply round to face the front door and commanded the footman to call their chairs.

The man was bewildered by this strange guest who wanted to leave directly he arrived. Rosalba could see the other footman laughing behind his hand. She had just begun to realize how badly she was behaving, but she was still fired by an inner desperation, and she was not the girl to give in to threats.

She wriggled out of Hugh's grasp, slipped past him and started to climb the stairs. She did realize vaguely that if she entered a room full of their friends as an absurd parody of

92

a scarlet woman, Hugh might find it hard to forgive her. She did not care—and she was craven enough to feel that she would rather face that crowd of people than go home with him in his present mood.

"Rosalba!" He was coming after her.

She glanced back over her shoulder, and it was her undoing. This was the staircase they had climbed on her very first entry into London life as Hugh's mistress; it rose out of the hall with a dramatic sweep. She was in a highly nervous state and the heat of the candles was oppressive; as she looked downwards and saw the drop to the floor below, she was seized by one of those fits of giddiness common in the first months of pregnancy. There was a thundering in her ears; light and sensation fled away from her and she was submerged in darkness.

The next thing she knew, she was lying on something that felt like a sofa in some place that was dim with dusk. The strains of music were still faintly audible but much further off. Two people were talking, a man and a woman. The man was Hugh.

"Are you sure?" he was saying. "Did she confide in you?"

"Not a word. There was no need. There is something in the face one can always recognize. Something about the eyes."

This was the melodious voice of Polly Palmer.

"But why didn't she tell me?"

"I expect she was afraid you would be displeased and say it was her fault."

"How could I be such a hypocrite? We are both equally responsible."

"Not many men will admit as much, my dear Rainham. They blame their wives for being barren and their mistresses for being fertile. I daresay she was trying to put off the evil day as long as possible. Perhaps that is why she is wearing such a lavish amount of rouge," added Polly doubtfully.

"No, she put that on to annoy me because I had been unkind and unfeeling. Poor Rosalba. Poor little girl."

There was such an aching tenderness in his voice that Rosalba opened her eyes and found herself gazing straight up into his.

"Did I faint? How silly of me."

93

She was immediately offered Polly's vinaigrette, a glass of water or a glass of champagne. She declined them all, saying she would soon be perfectly recovered. Polly had already undone her laces. She propped a cushion behind Rosalba's head and then went back to the concert and left the lovers alone. Hugh sat beside Rosalba on the sofa, holding her hand.

"Why didn't you tell me you were going to have a child?"

"I suppose I kept hoping it wasn't true. What on earth are we to do with it?"

"Do? Why, love it and care for it, of course. That is what people generally do with children."

"I shall get fat and ugly and you won't like me anymore. And how can we keep a child in Hunsden Street? There is no room for a nursery, and anyway it would be quite unsuitable. All your friends would laugh."

"Never mind my friends," said Hugh. "As for making any domestic changes, we need not think about them for some time yet—the child will be put out to nurse to begin with, won't it? More to the point, what are we to do with you for the next few months? I can see now why you would not go to Margaret. Babies are too distressing a subject for her, aren't they?"

Rosalba had not considered this, and felt a little ashamed of her selfishness.

"I tell you what," he continued. "I'll rent a house in some secluded place where we can spend the summer together."

"But you are going to Yorkshire!"

"I'll have to spend a week or two up there, but I won't leave you for long."

He bent and kissed her, acquiring a good smear of rouge in the process. She took his handkerchief and wiped it off his lips.

"You do look a perfect fright, my dear," he told her with loving severity. "And I can't think why you should be afraid of anything that childbearing can do to spoil your beauty. You are never likely to be more horribly disguised than you are at this moment."

PART TWO

AN HONORABLE ESTATE

1

Rosalba kept very well throughout her pregnancy. The early months were spent at a quiet, almost rural spa, the winter in Soho. Hugh remained at her side, and she lived in a sort of happy limbo. One possible cause of trouble was removed. John Meade, the lawyer, had formed the habit of visiting her every so often, and one day he brought the disturbing news that Carlow was back in England. Fortunately he was able to tell her a few days later that the Carlow family had made a final effort to be rid of him: they had paid his passage to the American Colonies.

Rosalba's daughter was born in March, and named Anne after her maternal grandmother. She was a pretty little baby with a fluff of dark hair and Hugh's hazel eyes. Rosalba found her strangely enchanting.

"I had no idea I should like her so much," she said, gazing down at the little sleeping doll in her arms. Her eyes filled with tears as she added, "How horrid and selfish I have been, not wanting her to be born. I wish I could keep her with me, instead of putting her out to nurse."

"I'm afraid that's hardly practical, my dear," said Hugh. "There really is not room in this house for a wet nurse and two children. Mrs. Bracey is wanting to return to her own family, and if she doesn't go soon, I think both the maids will leave. And you know little Anne will be much better off in the country air at Islington."

Mrs. Bracey was the excellent wet nurse who had been recommended by Polly Palmer. She had moved into Hunsden Street with her own baby the day after Rosalba's confinement; she was anxious to get back to her cottage in Islington, where her husband worked in a market garden.

"I shall be able to have her with me later?" asked Rosalba, begging for a concession she had never previously cared about.

"Of course you shall, my love," said Hugh, leaning across the bed to kiss her gently on the forehead. "As soon as the little girl is fit to be weaned, we'll make some new arrangements."

Rosalba had to be content with that. Before the child was removed to Islington, they took her to be christened in the parish church. This was not a happy occasion, as the officiating curate seized on the opportunity to admonish the child's parents for their sinful way of life. Rosalba burst into tears (she was still weak from her lying-in), while Hugh was so angry that he had to be almost forcibly dragged out of the church by Lord Retford, who had come to act as godfather.

"You can't assault a parson on consecrated ground, my dear fellow," he said firmly. "No matter how objectionable he may be."

"Damn his sanctimonious impudence! I paid him to baptize my daughter, not to teach me morality and upset Rosalba. Why can't these people mind their own business?"

"I suppose he thought it *was* his business," said Rosalba. She could not help being amused by Hugh's attitude, and this made her feel better.

Then Anne was driven off to Islington, and everything seemed suddenly flat.

Although she soon recovered her physical health and looks, Rosalba was in low spirits. Besides missing her baby, she had begun, rather belatedly, to feel guilty about the life she was leading. The disapproving clergyman had merely put into words ideas that were already forcing their way into her mind. Like most new-made mothers, she had felt a great longing for her own mother, and she kept imagining what Mama would have felt about her present situation. The picture of herself as a kept woman with a bastard child was made all the more painful by the recollection that Mama had actually been born to the same fate as little Anne. Carlow had revealed this secret on what turned out to be the last day that he and Rosalba spent together: the elder Anne had not been entirely abandoned, she had been given a good education and a modest dowry and enabled to marry an army officer—but essentially she had lived a precarious life without family connections, and who was to say that her grandchild's future would be any safer?

Suppose I was to die? thought Rosalba. Or suppose Hugh

was to marry? The idea terrified her, and knowing that he would always provide for them materially was a poor consolation.

She had to hide these fears from Hugh; repeating them to a man who had been so loving and generous to her would be not only ungrateful but downright stupid, and if she hadn't realized this already, a letter from Margaret would have been warning enough.

After months of suspecting St. John Roche of infidelity every time he went out of her sight, she had at last caught him in bed with her maid. He had been heartless and impenitent, blamed Margaret for nagging him to death, said that he was entitled to amuse himself and if the girl was sent away he would go as well. After some hysterical scenes, Margaret had been forced to accept this degrading *ménage à trois*. She could not face an existence without Roche, she wrote. Adding bleakly, "I have done wrong and I am being punished for it."

"Oh, poor Margaret!" Rosalba exclaimed aloud to the empty room. It was painful to recall their first meeting, her admiring interest in Margaret and Roche. Was this where a totally reckless and single-minded love led in the end?

She was still feeling very despondent when her footman Tobias announced: "Mr. Meade."

He generally came when she was likely to be alone; she thought he was afraid of some of her less respectable callers. He had brought a book of essays with him—hoped it would interest her—then he changed the subject abruptly.

"You are distressed. Can you tell me what is the matter?"

"It is nothing. A sad letter from a friend, that is all."

"And perhaps you miss your little daughter?"

Surprised by his perception, she admitted this was true.

"It's monstrous," he said indignantly, "that she should have been torn from your arms—"

"You exaggerate," said Rosalba, now wanting to giggle at this extravagance. "We had to put her out to nurse, you know. The air of Islington—"

"She had to be got out of Rainham's way, I suppose. He must be utterly selfish and unfeeling! It stands to reason; no man with an ounce of sensibility would compel you to live here like a caged bird—I know you are always loyal to him, but you are not happy. If only you would let me take you away, take care of you—"

He was fully launched on a declaration of romantic love. Rosalba sat in dumb astonishment. Why do I never see these things coming? she wondered distractedly. John Meade's ideal passion surprised her just as much as St. John Roche's unscrupulous lust had done. Was this because she never really saw any man properly except Hugh?

She did manage to stop the flow of Meade's eloquence at last, and pretty sharply.

"I don't want to hear any more of that nonsense," she told him. "I think you had better leave now, and I would rather not see you again. I am sorry if this gives you pain, but you had no right to come here and act such a scene!"

"I know I should not have spoken. It was only because I found you in such despair—"

"I was not in despair!" she contradicted him, very much annoyed. "And before you make any more unjust and impertinent charges against Mr. Rainham, let me remind you that he has done everything in his power to make me happy. There is only one thing lacking in my life, and you could not provide that either. You cannot offer to become my husband, even supposing you wished to. I am married already."

This seemed to crush him utterly, and she recognized that he really had not meant to come out with any of those sentiments: they were the outcome of dreams and desires which he had probably been suppressing for some time. Of course he knew he could do nothing for her which Hugh was not doing more effectively.

So she sent him away with a genuine sense of pity, seeing him so humble and hangdog, and because of this she did not tell Hugh she had received a dishonorable proposal from her respectable legal friend. Whether he was annoyed at Meade's presumption or simply amused, it would not be fair to tell the story without explaining that he had only given way to this outburst after finding her on the verge of tears. And naturally she did not want Hugh to know that.

As it turned out, she started to feel a good deal more cheerful during the next fortnight and now looked back on her fit of moping as an extraordinary weakness, so that when John Meade called on her again, she was neither pleased nor sympathetic.

She was crossing the hall just as Tobias opened the front door. Seeing who it was, she stopped and said, "What are you doing here?"

"If I might speak to you, Mrs. York—"

"I told you to keep away."

Meade was constrained by the presence of Tobias, being more easily embarrassed than Rosalba.

He said, with a meaningful glance at the footman, "There is something of an urgent nature I should like to discuss with you privately. It has to do with your—with Mr. Edgar Carlow."

This shook her a little. Any mention of her husband always sounded like bad news, and now she came to look at John Meade more closely, he was plainly in a high state of agitation. Perhaps he had come to warn her of some impending disaster.

"Very well," she said. "I can see you for a few minutes, but I am going out soon; I am expecting Mr. Rainham to fetch me."

She led him into the eating room. As usual, when there was no meal in progress, the table had been folded and moved away and the chairs ranged along the wall, leaving an open space in the middle of the floor. Rosalba and Meade sat down on two of the chairs, side by side.

"Tell me the worst," she said. "What has Carlow done now?"

"He has been drowned."

"You mean he is dead?" Which was, she thought afterwards, a very silly thing to say, for what else could he mean? "How do you know? How did it happen and where?"

"Crossing the Atlantic on his passage to America. There was a storm and he was swept overboard."

"But that was months ago! You told me that his family had paid for him to go to the Colonies back in the autumn."

"Yes, and the ship he sailed on has only recently returned to her home port. The captain arrived at my chambers yesterday, to report the accident and to hand over poor Carlow's effects."

She listened while Meade gave her all the details; a violent storm in mid-ocean, the passengers obliged to remain below for days on end, Carlow venturing on deck (against advice), the angle of the ship, the slippery boards, the force of the wind, his being carried away by a great wave. She heard it all as though it had been some far-off traveler's tale, quite removed from herself.

"It was kind of you to come and tell me," she said when he had finished.

"You know I would do anything for you. Anything in the world."

He looked so earnest that she thought he was about to declare his love for her all over again, so she managed to imply, rather meanly, that this was hardly the time for a display of such emotions. John Meade was so correct that he would never willingly commit a lapse of taste, and left at once, only begging that he might be allowed to call again in a week or two. She hadn't the heart to refuse.

Hugh, arriving ten minutes later, found her still in the eating parlor.

"What are you doing in here, my love, sitting like Patience on a monument? Is something the matter?"

When she told him, he stood quite still for a moment, as though collecting his thoughts. Then he pulled round another of the straight-backed chairs and sat down, almost touching her.

"You're not grieving for him?"

"Oh no! How could I be such a hypocrite? Only it does seem dreadful that I should feel so indifferent to the death of a man I married less than two years ago."

"That's not your fault. He did not allow you any natural scope for your affection. He used you as a pawn, and what seems to be almost as bad, he never even tried to disguise the fact."

This was certainly true.

"I don't wish to be hasty or indelicate," said Hugh. "Yet any pretense of mourning would, as you say, be sheer hy-

101

pocrisy. And apparently you have actually been a widow for several months, even if you didn't know it."

She gazed at him in perplexity. "Why should you be indelicate? What are you talking about?"

"I am wondering if it is too soon for you to consider a second marriage."

"A second—Hugh, you are not—you cannot be making me an offer?"

He seemed surprised by her surprise.

"Of course I am," he said. "What else did you expect? You know I love you, or you ought to know by this time. I have been wanting to marry you ever since the day I had to chase you up that dark alley in Spitalfields."

"You never said so."

"No," he agreed. "We couldn't marry while you had a husband living, and I don't see much sense in crying for the unattainable. It so often spoils the happiness one can attain. But did you not consider what might happen if Carlow died?"

She shook her head. Carlow's death had never really entered her mind as being at all likely; he was too much of a proverbial bad penny. And besides, men like Hugh Rainham seldom married their mistresses. By living with him openly and accepting his money, she thought she had put herself beyond the pale.

When she tried to say all this, Hugh brushed it aside and told her not to talk like a character in a moralizing novel.

"Of course I am going to marry you. It may be awkward at first, I agree, but a little awkwardness is not an impassable barrier. My family will come round in time. No family that includes Gus can afford to be too censorious, after all. And my real friends will accept you and love you. If there are some people who don't care to meet you, I am sure we shall do very well without them."

"Yet you have always said that Margaret could never have resumed her old place in society, even if Roche had been able to marry her."

"No, and for a good reason. Sooner or later she and Roche and George Lodney would all have found themselves in the same company—a woman with two husbands above ground, and on an identical piece of ground at that! It is a kind of situation that makes people very uncomfortable. So they won't put up with it. There's no impediment of that sort where you and I are concerned. I suppose our marriage will cause a nine days' wonder; I'm not suggesting you should plunge straight away into the complexities of becoming a lady of fashion. I have been thinking for some time that I should like to take you abroad, to France and Italy perhaps. Why shouldn't we make it a wedding trip?"

Still she hesitated, looking into his keen, clever face; his eyes were smiling as he set himself to persuade her. She struggled against temptation, sensing that this decision ought to be delayed and considered more carefully.

"Don't put on that proud expression and turn me down. Unless," he added with a sudden and disarming diffidence, "unless you don't want to marry me."

"Oh, but I do. You must know I do. More than anything in the world."

2

Having won his point, Hugh was determined to go ahead as quickly as possible. They were to be married by licence in ten days' time, and the carriage that waited for them outside the church would take them straight off on the first stage of their journey to the Continent.

Hugh broke the news to his sister, though he did not tell Rosalba how she had taken it, which was probably a bad omen. He wrote to various other relations, but made no attempt to notify Gus. They had not met or corresponded since the violent scene in Grosvenor Street nearly a year ago. Gus had become increasingly debauched and his gaming losses were mounting; he no longer moved in the society to which he and his wife had been born, nor even in the easygoing, less exclusive but perfectly civilized circle where Rosalba had her friends. Gus, it seemed, had sunk to a lower level.

As they were closing the house in Hunsden Street, Rosalba felt obliged to find new places for her three servants. She also drove out to Islington to see her baby, who was to be left with the Braceys while her parents were abroad. With so much to be done, and all the excitments of shopping and packing, she almost overlooked one letter that ought to be written. It seemed only right, in the circumstances, to let John Meade know she was going to be married. She had a strong suspicion that he was intending to make her an offer himself, and she wanted to save him from the unnecessary pain of being refused.

She received his reply on the morning of her wedding day while she was getting dressed with the admiring help of her two maids. The letter was ominously thick; she tore it open and found two pages crammed with writing—this was no civil note of congratulations, and from the few words that caught her eyes, all concerned with anxiety, sorrow and desperation, she guessed that he was going through the attitudes of a rejected lover. Well, she had no time for that kind of thing. She dropped the letter on the table and it slid onto the floor, where it was submerged in a sea of crumpled paper, torn-up invitations, broken fans and other rubbish that was to be thrown away.

Hugh had arrived to fetch her; she ran downstairs into his arms, in her beautiful new morning gown of glazed oriental cotton all over tiny pagodalike patterns in blue and yellow on a white ground. Her chip-straw hat was a kind of pagoda too.

"You look adorable," said Hugh, kissing her. "My lovely bride."

They held hands on the way to St. George's Hanover Square. Hugh had decided that they should be married at his parish church, thus avoiding the parson he disliked so much in Soho. They had agreed that the wedding should be entirely private—so that they could get away immediately afterwards, Hugh said. The real reason, she suspected, was to spare her the embarrassment of being made an honest woman while anyone she knew was looking on.

He would send a notice to the newspapers, announcing his marriage to "the Widow of the late Edgar Carlow Esquire."

"That will be quite a puzzle to some people," said Rosalba, amused.

They had now arrived at the church, and as he handed her

out of the carriage, Hugh admitted that he had told his sister the time of the wedding, though he did not think she would be present.

Olivia Rainham was not in the church, to Rosalba's secret relief. The marriage was as quiet and private as she had hoped: she was given away by the clerk, who with the sexton afterwards signed the register.

As they came down the aisle in a state of silent emotion, a tall woman in green stepped out from behind the last pew.

"So you did come after all, Livy," said Hugh. "You are just in time to wish us joy."

His sister did not seem to have heard him. She said, "The most dreadful thing has happened. I promised Alicia I would find you. Gus is dead. He was taken ill suddenly, as far as I can make out, and died during the night."

Hugh did not speak for a minute. Rosalba could read his expression like a book. On our wedding day, he seemed to be thinking. What a time to choose—and how exactly like Gus.

Making the necessary effort, he said conventionally, "I am sorry to hear it. Poor fellow. What does Dr. Baker say? I suppose Alicia sent for him?"

"No, you don't understand! Gus wasn't in Grosvenor Street, that is what is so dreadful. He hasn't been home for a few days. Alicia didn't know where he was; in one of his horrid, low haunts, gaming or worse. And this morning she received a message from a woman who keeps a disorderly house near Covent Garden, saying that Sir Augustus Rainham was dead and would her ladyship kindly arrange for the removal of his body. Alicia fainted from the shock, and the servants sent for me to go to her."

"Oh, my God," said Hugh under his breath.

He must have seen what was coming.

"You will have to go and deal with these people, Hugh. Recover Gus's body and get the whole thing hushed up with as little scandal as possible."

"But I've just been married!" protested the bridegroom, with less than his usual resolution. "We're on our way to France."

"Then perhaps you will tell me who else I can turn to? Uncle Robert and William are both in Derbyshire, and such a delicate matter should not be left to servants or even lawyers. One of the family ought to deal with it. Are you suggesting that Alicia should go and collect her husband's body from a house of ill repute?"

Rosalba pressed Hugh's arm, saying, "Poor Lady Alicia, how very distressed she must be. I think you ought to do what is required."

"Yes, I'm afraid I ought," he said, glancing down at her. And to his sister, "Have you the address?"

She handed him a slip of paper. He read it, frowning.

"Of all the dens of iniquity! It could hardly be worse. I think I'll go there on foot. You had better take the carriage and wait for me."

It was not absolutely clear which of his womenfolk he was talking to. A few minutes later both Rosalba and Olivia were in the traveling chaise, being driven towards the house in Pall Mall.

It was clear that Olivia resented her new sister-in-law. At first Rosalba felt inclined to apologize for her existence, then she decided that this was ridiculous. She was now Hugh's wife; the carriage they were driving in and the house they were going to were both included among the worldly goods with which he had just endowed her. She sat quietly with her hands in her lap, gazing out of the window.

Olivia asked suspiciously, "Are you acquainted with this woman?"

"Which woman?"

"The person who keeps the house where my cousin died?"

Rosalba stared at her in growing incredulity.

"No, I am not," she said at last. "I realize that a lady of your irreproachable virtue is inclined to look down on all forms of human frailty from a great height, and that you hardly discriminate between them. All the same, I think you should know your own brother well enough to know that he wouldn't marry a girl out of a brothel. I don't care what you think of me, but I won't have you insulting Hugh."

Olivia turned as red as a turkey, pursed her mouth and said no more. When they reached the house in Pall Mall she went immediately upstairs and left Rosalba in the hall, perhaps intending to embarrass her: the wife who did not know her way around her husband's house.

But Rosalba remembered where the library was from her previous visit; she went in there and sat down to wait for Hugh.

She had to wait nearly three hours.

The butler came in presently and asked her with great respect if she would like any refreshment. She refused, but later was glad to accept a slice of cold meat and a glass of wine. She became restless and finally apprehensive. What on earth could Hugh be doing?

At last she heard sounds of an arrival. She hurried into the hall, to meet Hugh just coming in, with Lady Alicia Rainham leaning on his arm and looking distracted and disheveled, with a hat jammed on over her lace cap at a very odd angle. There was a servant carrying cloaks and dressing cases and other paraphernalia as though she was meaning to stay, which seemed rather peculiar, and a nursemaid carrying little Theodore, now aged fourteen months. He had been named after the Nabob.

"Rosalba!" exclaimed Hugh, who was obviously thankful to see her. "Will you look after my cousin? Yes, take her into the library. Where is Olivia?"

"She went upstairs."

Hugh left Rosalba alone, for the second time that day, with one of her new relations.

Gus's widow showed no signs of outraged propriety; she was far too upset. And perhaps she does not realize who I am, thought Rosalba, as she made a stiff little speech of condolence.

But Lady Alicia did know, for she said faintly, "You are very kind. And I am afraid I have spoiled your plans. Only it is all so very dreadful and I didn't know which way to turn. And I expect Olivia will hold me to blame."

"That would be quite unjust," exclaimed Rosalba, who suddenly perceived that she and this aristocratic young woman had something in common: they had both been the helpless victims of unsatisfactory husbands. She said, "Miss Rainham is in no position to judge. She has never been married."

"No, she hasn't," agreed Lady Alicia, brightening a little. "It is absurd for her to pretend she understands everything.

I did try very hard to get poor Gus to behave sensibly, but he never would listen. And it's not as though I had any idea what he was doing."

This struck Rosalba as distinctly odd, considering that everyone else in London seemed to have known exactly what the wretched Gus was doing.

Hugh and Olivia now came into the library together.

"I could not leave Alicia in Grosvenor Street," Hugh was saying.

"Why not?" asked Olivia. "Naturally I am delighted to have her here with little Theo—you know that, my dear Alicia, I am sure. But what prevented their remaining in their own house?"

"The duns have taken up residence in the front hall."

"Good God, I had not realized matters had gone so far—that stupid, feckless boy! Even so, to arrive on the day of his death—I call that positively indecent."

Hugh began to explain, leaving some things unsaid, out of consideration for Alicia, though the facts were not difficult to follow. For years Gus had been an addicted gamester and not a very clever one, losing more than he won. He had been obliged to settle his gaming losses immediately. To pay these so-called debts of honor, he had borrowed from professional moneylenders, who charged an extortionately high interest. The usurers had not pressed for repayment, knowing that Gus had great resources behind him, and the longer his debts ran on, the more they stood to gain—until just lately, when his creditors had begun to suspect that his liabilities might have outgrown his assets. When he had been taken ill several days ago at the disreputable house near Covent Garden, the news had spread among the gaming and moneylending fraternity before it reached his own family, with the result that the vultures were gathering in full force, each determined to bully and cajole as much as he could out of the widow, guessing that the young heir's trustees would be far more intransigent.

"Though I suppose they will have to be paid in the end," said Olivia. "Will Liston have to go? I do think, Alicia, you could have done more to overcome Gus's insane passion for gaming."

Alicia began to cry, and Rosalba realized that she had been talking about her husband's accumulating debts rather than his visits to brothels when she said she had not known what he was doing.

"What is to become of us?" she sobbed. "We shall be quite ruined and my little Theo will be a pauper."

"No, he won't," said Hugh. "Not so long as he has Ashwin and the rest of the Derbyshire property. Gus could not touch that, you know. It is all entailed. The best thing will be for you and Theo to go and live up there, very quietly and inexpensively, and away from Gus's creditors, until matters have been sorted out. I take it he left a will—the lawyers will have seen to that—and if he appointed a guardian for his son, I expect it will be my Uncle Robert. He will take good care of you both."

"No," said Alicia, through her tears.

"You don't wish to have him as your adviser? He is very kindhearted, as well as being practical and shrewd."

"Yes, I know." She looked up at him through drowned violet eyes. "I did not mean that I have anything against General Rainham, only that he is not the person named as Theo's guardian. You are."

Hugh stared at her with a mixture of disbelief and dismay.

"But my dear girl, it's not possible. You know Gus hated me. Since we had that quarrel last year—"

"He said he was going to alter his will, but he never did. I'm sure of it, for a few weeks ago that old man who owns the bank came to call. I think he must have been trying to remonstrate with Gus about the debts, though I didn't realize it at the time. I thought he was talking about the rakish life Gus was leading, when he said, 'What will become of your son, Sir Augustus, if you should die while he is still a child?' And Gus said, 'He'll have my upright cousin Hugh to keep him on the straight and narrow path, and perhaps he'll be better off than I was.'"

There was a dead silence in the library, and for the first time Rosalba felt a genuine pang of pity for the troublesome, dissolute and singularly unattractive young man who had wasted his life and fortune and died in Hogarthian squalor at the age of twenty-four. Somewhere at the back of his weak and fuddled mind there must have been the idea that he himself had lost his way; he would never admit this directly or try to reform; he would not or could not put up any sort of struggle against the tide of self-indulgence that had finally overwhelmed him—yet he had dimly felt that he wanted something different for his young son. Perhaps this was a saving grace.

"And I don't see how I can refuse to act," Hugh said to Rosalba when at last they were alone. "If that poor silly creature trusted me to take care of his boy, in spite of disliking me so much and never attending to a word I said—who but Gus could behave so inconsistently?"

"Perhaps if he knew he was ruined—did he realize that?"

"I think he must have done. The woman at the bordello told me he kept begging her not to notify any of the family after he became ill."

"What did he die of? I hardly liked to ask before."

"He had a heavy cold which turned to an inflammation of the lungs; that was what killed him, assisted by brandy and the pox—though I think we need not mention the latter in front of Alicia; she has enough to put up with already." Hugh paused and glanced rather anxiously at his bride. "The thing is, my love, I don't feel I ought to leave the country at present. I think I must convey Alicia and the child to Derbyshire and look into matters up there with Robinson, the land agent."

He paused again. Did he expect her to make a scene? She had already guessed what was going to happen, so she was able to hide her disappointment.

"Of course you will have to go to Derbyshire. May I come with you?"

"I want you to come. I am afraid it will be a somewhat gloomy occasion, but at least we shall be together."

3

"What do you think?" Lettice Rainham confided to her friend Dorothy Lumm. "My cousin Hugh is going to marry his mistress—I suppose he has actually done so by now. The family are in such a taking—you can't imagine!"

Miss Lumm, being several years older than Lettice, felt she ought to set an example either of pious horror or worldly wisdom, but could not decide which.

So she said what she actually thought. "How excessively romantic!"

"Yes, isn't it? For she is the prettiest, most elegant creature. I saw her at Liston—I think I told you. She is a widow, quite young and not at all vulgar."

"What is her name?"

Lettice had to admit she did not know. "No one will ever tell me about her; they try to pretend I didn't meet her, which is silly. Hugh calls her something poetical like Rosalind or Pamela—William let me know that much—and Cousin Olivia always speaks of her as That Woman."

"I don't think Pamela sounds very suitable," said Dorothy, recalling the heroine of Richardson's famous novel. "She spent her time refusing the wicked enticements of Mr. B."

Both the girls laughed. They were sitting in the morning room of the Lumms' house in Trilbourne, with a clear view across the sunlit High Street. Trilbourne in Derbyshire was a flourishing country town which besides a fine parish church, a market, a cluster of decent shops and plenty of dwellings for people of the middling and lower sort also had some fine houses occupied by families of consequence. Most of these had been built about sixty or seventy years ago. The badness of the roads in those days, and the heavy snowdrifts that were common in this hilly country, made winter a bleak time for the local gentry if they remained in their isolated halls and manors, so many of them built themselves town houses and occupied them for several months each year. Some families still did this, but Bridge Place, the town house of the Rainhams of Ashwin Hall, was now occupied permanently by Lettice's parents, General and Mrs. Robert Rainham. Opposite the Lumms was the house of Mr. Sturdy, the antiquarian. Glancing out of the window, Lettice could see this high solid building of gray stone, with its steep roof and narrow, old-fashioned windows.

"Are we likely to see this shocking new relation of yours?" inquired Dorothy, picking up her tambour work.

"I'm afraid not. They are going abroad to avoid the scandal. Isn't it a pity?"

"She seems a very fortunate young woman. I should like to go abroad on my wedding tour."

I daresay you will, thought Lettice, and perhaps quite soon. Dorothy was an heiress. Her mother had grown up in Trilbourne, the daughter of a former rector. Although perfectly wellborn she had no fortune and had been glad to marry a wealthy but ungenteel Mr. Lumm, the master of a Birmingham brass foundry. The marriage had been happy enough, though after his death Mrs. Lumm had moved back to Derbyshire so that she could bring up her only child in more agreeable surroundings. With her mother's breeding and her father's money, Dorothy was a catch, a tall, lively girl, not pretty but with a fine figure and a glowing complexion. Quite recently she had met a man who had taken her fancy.

When Lettice got up to leave, Dorothy decided to walk as far as Bridge Place with her. As they emerged into the street, a slim young man with an air of great elegance strolled into sight on the opposite pavement.

"Do you see who is coming our way?" whispered Lettice.

Dorothy certainly did see, but she let her gaze travel on to a less imposing figure.

"Do you mean Mr. Dan Robinson?"

"Lord, no! Who cares for him? I mean your admirer, Ned Chivers."

The two men had now met; they stopped to greet each other and then crossed the road together to speak to the young ladies. There were bows and smiles and inquiries.

"If you are going to Bridge Place," the young man called Chivers said to Dorothy Lumm, "perhaps we may accompany you?"

She agreed, blushing faintly with pleasure, and they fell into step, talking with great animation. He was very handsome with his fair, regular good looks, thought Lettice as she followed with Mr. Robinson.

Lettice's romantic interest in people like her cousin Hugh and his unsuitable wife did not extend as far as Dan Robinson, the scapegrace younger brother of the Ashwin land agent. She thought him a common little man. However dashingly wicked his exploits might be in London or Paris, his returns to his family in Trilbourne were usually made when he was short of funds and rather subdued; he would never try to flirt with or impress the daughter of General Rainham. They conversed somewhat stiffly.

"Do you know how much longer Mr. Chivers is likely to remain in Trilbourne?" she asked him.

"I'm afraid not, Miss Lettice. I am not in his confidence. Though I gather from my brother that he is thinking of buying an estate in these parts. He has been consulting George, as I daresay you know, about the price of land, and farming conditions generally. That is how we first became acquainted."

Lettice knew this much already. A charming young man in easy circumstances, looking for somewhere to settle, was naturally a person of interest in a place like Trilbourne, and as he had now been here more than a month, it did seem as though he was greatly attracted by the neighborhood or Dorothy Lumm, probably both.

By now they had reached Bridge Place, the best house in Trilbourne, which stood in its own grounds, a little apart from the rest of the town and overlooking the shining water of the River Tirrel, glassy-smooth and transparent here, just above the ancient stone bridge.

Lettice invited her companions into the house. They entered the saloon, which was dim and cool, the curtains drawn against the invading sun. She had hardly seated her guests with what she considered was the proper dignity of a hostess when her mother spoiled the effect by coming into the room in a high state of agitation.

"A messenger has just come from Hugh, riding post all the way, to tell your father that Gus was taken ill last week and

113

died within a few days. It seems incredible. He was only twenty-four."

"Poor Gus!" exclaimed Lettice. "How dreadful."

She had never been at all fond of him, but he was young enough to make his death seem a tragedy, and she was young enough to be affected by anyone's death as something solemn and unusual.

"And Hugh is bringing Alicia and Little Theodore up here and I suppose will have to stay in this house, for Ashwin is certainly not fit to receive them."

Mrs. Rainham, flurried and voluble, only now appeared to notice her daughter's friends. They had all risen when she came in, and the two men were exchanging signs and glances, as though feeling they ought to withdraw. Dorothy saw this, and felt it was up to her to make the first move.

"I am so very sorry to hear your sad news, ma'am," she said, "and I know my mama will be equally distressed. We won't keep Lettice talking any longer, for I am sure you will want to be alone."

She thought she ought to have paid some sort of tribute to Sir Augustus but could not for the life of her think what. The men helped her out with their own civil condolences, and they all made their escape. The baronet's death had cast an unexpectedly dark shadow over the morning, and neither of Dorothy's companions had much to say on their return through the town. She found them uncommonly stupid.

4

"I daresay you are not much accustomed to country life," General Rainham remarked to Rosalba as she sat on his left at dinner.

He was a thin, upright man, his face reddened by sun and wind rather than good living, and he had received his nephew's wife into his house very correctly if without much warmth.

Rosalba told him she had grown up in Suffolk. "My father

was obliged to leave the army after being severely wounded in Canada."

"So your father was a military man. What was his rank?"

"He was a captain, sir."

"In which regiment?"

She told him, and saw him assessing the likelihood of this in his mind. He thought she was lying. Boasting of an imaginary gentility, because the truth was too sordid to reveal. She had a sudden desire to behave as vulgarly as possible and confirm his worst fears. Mrs. Rainham had provided a magnificent dinner to revive the travelers from London after a long and weary journey. The first course included fifteen different dishes. It would be amusing, Rosalba thought, to insist on having her plate piled high with a little of everything that was going, to make an outcry about wanting the broiled trout or the pickled brawn from the far end of the table, as though she had never been at a gentleman's dinner table before. But she knew she must not disgrace Hugh, who had just sent her an encouraging smile from his place beside his aunt. Conducting herself like a lady, she accepted moderate helpings of chicken, asparagus and braised ham from the three dishes nearest to her, and made polite conversation with William Rainham, the general's son, who sat on her other side. He was very attentive, and perhaps it was stupid to suppose that he was waiting for her to drop her aitches or her fork.

At least the general and his son were pleasant neighbors at dinner. When the women retired to the drawing room, Rosalba's position became more uncomfortable. Olivia, assuming control, established herself and her aunt in one corner of the room, with Alicia between them, so that they could discuss the problems caused by Gus's death. Rosalba was left to find herself a chair outside this charmed triangle.

Only Lettice Rainham took any notice of her, saying with a smile, "Last time we met you had been skating on the lake at Liston."

Yes, but we are all supposed to pretend that such an encounter never took place, thought Rosalba.

She said, "I saw another stretch of water from my window before dinner. That is not a lake?"

"No, it is the River Tirrel. There is some very romantic scenery round about, which I can show you if you are fond of walking."

Olivia had been watching them. She said something in a low voice to her aunt.

"Lettice," said Mrs. Rainham, "will you go up and make sure that Cousin Alicia's nursemaid has everything she needs? And then you can help Miller look out our black gloves; we had plenty of pairs put by after Grandmama died."

"Yes, Mama," said Lettice, reluctant but obedient.

It was plain that she was being got out of the way of Hugh's wicked wife. Rosalba sat by herself, ignored by her companions. Alicia glanced at her occasionally; she was quite prepared to be friendly and during the journey she had always turned to Rosalba in preference to Olivia. But Alicia was timid at the best of times, and at present she was exhausted and frightened by a sequence of calamities; she could not exert herself on Rosalba's account. Hugh's sister and aunt ignored his wife so completely that they might as well have sent her to sit in the servants' hall. Only then, of course, she would have corrupted the housemaids.

It was a very long, dull evening.

When the tea table was set, she was silently offered a cup. She sipped the straw-colored liquid, glad of something to do with her hands. She had hoped for some improvement when the gentlemen joined them, but they never came. Understandably, they too were having a conference.

They were still in the library when the ladies went upstairs. Rosalba undressed in the large unfamiliar room that she and Hugh had been given; she had been lying alone for an hour in the big tester bed before he finally arrived, looking preoccupied.

"Matters are even worse than I thought," he said. "That little monster has milked the estate of every penny he could get—I know I shouldn't call him that now he's dead, but he really did behave like a lunatic. He squandered the entire rent roll, sold off timber and never replanted, never repaired so much as a broken gate. If everything else has to go to pay his debts—and I'm very much afraid it will—we are going

116

to have the devil of a struggle getting the entailed property back into reasonable shape."

"We?" she inquired suspiciously.

"Myself and George Robinson." Hugh sat down on the bed and took her hand. "I'm sorry, my love. It seems I shall be forced to remain here for the next few months. There are too many difficult decisions to be made, and I can't leave them to George; he hasn't the confidence or the authority."

"Could not your uncle support and advise Mr. Robinson? I know you are little Theo's trustee, but it is the general who lives on the spot—"

"My uncle is most unwilling to become involved. He is very awkwardly placed. Theo seems a healthy child, considering his parentage, but he is very young and comes of delicate stock. If he were to die, it is my uncle who would succeed, and after him William. Don't you see how bad it would look to Alicia if he was continually preaching economy and refusing her requests for money because every penny is needed to spend on the estate—an estate which in the long run may benefit his son rather than hers?"

Rosalba did not think Alicia was the sort of person who would become aware of such underlying motives, but the general obviously was, and she could understand his scruples.

"I'm sorry," said Hugh again. "Do you mind very much? We shall have our Continental tour eventually, I promise you."

Rosalba felt like saying that she was not a spoiled child lamenting over a postponed treat; what she disliked was the prospect of living for several months in a house where everyone resented and despised her. When he asked her to marry him, Hugh had admitted that there would be some awkwardness before she was accepted as his wife—this had been the original reason for their planning to go abroad. Now, in the crisis created by Gus's death, he had either forgotten, or he simply failed to notice his relations' hostility.

She felt a strong sense of grievance, but something restrained her from telling him so. Perhaps she was still haunted by the awful warning of poor Margaret Lodney, whose self-pity proved so destructive.

Next morning after breakfast Hugh was closeted in the
117

library with his uncle and the agent, George Robinson, so Rosalba went for a stroll round the garden, ending up at a pretty little orangery built onto the side of the house, where she sat down on a stone bench in the open doorway, to enjoy the sweet and spicy scents of many exotic plants, the lacy pattern of sunlight drifting down through the leaves of an ancient vine, and the view across the lawn to some woods on the far side of the river.

The river itself lay below her level of vision, but there was a path leading in that direction and perhaps providing a shortcut from the town, for presently she saw coming towards her someone who was not one of the inhabitants of Bridge Place: an elderly gentleman in blue broadcloth, with a long old-fashioned wig that looked rather hot for him on such a fine morning. He had a stick which he leaned on as he walked, though he seemed otherwise quite active.

When he reached the orangery, he took off his hat, made Rosalba a courtly bow, and said, "Am I right in supposing, ma'am, that you are Mrs. Hugh Rainham?"

"Yes, you are quite right, sir," she replied.

"I thought you must be Hugh's bride, for I see you are in mourning. My name is Henry Sturdy, though I don't expect you have ever heard of me."

"Indeed I have, sir. My husband has often spoken of you."

This was the wealthy antiquarian who had once tried to rent Ashwin in order to carry out some badly needed restoration; Gus had refused his offer, she remembered, for no other reason than to annoy Hugh.

"I have come to pay my call of condolence on Lady Alicia," said Mr. Sturdy. "That is, I shall leave my card only. I don't expect anyone to receive me—they will all be so much engaged. I came by the footpath on purpose, to avoid the noise of arriving in a carriage."

In spite of this thoughtful behavior, he looked rather wistfully at the house, as though he would like to know what was going on inside, and Rosalba invited him to sit on the stone bench and take a short rest after his walk. This pleased him, and soon they were talking away in a most friendly manner. Mr. Sturdy sat upright and foursquare, his walking stick laid across his knees. It was an unusual object, being made of ebony, with a handle curiously shaped like a silver hand clasping a ball of polished marble.

After touching on several topics and paying a handsome tribute to Hugh, whom he seemed to admire, the old man suddenly asked, "Am I right in supposing, madam, that you were formerly an actress?"

Rosalba felt a prickle of discomfort. He had treated her with such unaffected courtesy that she had imagined he was either unaware of her past history or too liberal to hold it against her. Now here he was with a sly hint about her being an actress, the profession often claimed by courtesans and prostitutes.

"No, sir," she said coldly. "I was never on the stage. Whatever else you may have heard of me."

Mr. Sturdy realized that he had offended her.

"Good God!" he exclaimed in a great fluster. "I had no intention—never meant to imply—my dear Mrs. Hugh, what must you think of me? It was entirely a bow at a venture, based on some rumor I heard and which I'm sure must have been a fallacy. I should so very much like to meet a lady who was acquainted with the characters of Juliet and Viola from the experience of actually playing them."

He gazed at her with a mixture of apology and disappointment, and she saw that she had misjudged him.

"I wish I could oblige you," she said with real regret. "What a pity I cannot introduce you to my friend Mrs. Polly Palmer. Are you very much interested in Shakespeare, sir?"

She soon realized that this question had been rather inept, for Mr. Sturdy was clearly a learned Shakespearean scholar and an enthusiast—he had written books on the subject. Even now he was on the verge of an exciting new quest.

"What would you say if his last, unfinished play was to be recovered, at this late date?"

"Was there such a play? I did not know."

"So it is conjectured. *The Noble History of King Arthur,* begun during his final years at Stratford—but I must not get on my hobbyhorse. And here is your husband."

Hugh had come round the corner of the house to look for her, and he and Mr. Sturdy were soon discussing all the problems connected with Gus's death.

The date for the burial could not be definitely fixed, since the coach bearing the coffin had not yet arrived. Traveling very slowly, it had left London before the family in their post chaises, and they had overtaken it on the way. In the meantime there was a great deal to do.

"I thought we would drive over to Ashwin presently," Hugh said to Rosalba.

Before she could answer, Mr. Sturdy said eagerly, "I wonder if I might meet you there? I am so very anxious to see the condition of the house."

Hugh and Rosalba were slightly taken aback; she knew he had wanted to go alone with her to his beloved Ashwin. But he was too courteous to let the antiquarian realize he had been tactless and at once agreed that he should join them.

"He cares so much for the house," said Hugh, when Mr. Sturdy had gone cheerfully off to order his carriage, "that I hadn't the heart to tell him I wanted to take you there on my own. We shall be able to make plenty of other solitary visits before the place is fit for Alicia to live in. And if we are going to have Sturdy with us this time, we might as well ask William and Lettice to come along too."

"I don't think your aunt will allow Lettice to come."

"Why not?" he asked. "Oh, I see. Well, I hope you are wrong, and I think you may be. It is my uncle who decides everything, and he is a man of the world. If he wants me to stay here and save him a lot of trouble, he must see to it that you are properly treated by his wife and daughter."

It was not perhaps the most encouraging way of making Rosalba feel welcome, but at least it was accurate: when they set off for Ashwin in William's phaeton, Lettice was with them, her eyes sparkling with anticipation under the brim of her summer hat.

"I am glad to have a chance of exploring the old house, for I suppose I shan't be able to make up a picnic party with Dorothy Lumm and Mr. Chivers, now we are in mourning."

"Who is Mr. Chivers?" asked Hugh.

"He is a very agreeable young man who is trying to buy an estate. I think he is in love with Dorothy."

They had left the town traffic behind and were now on an open stretch of road running parallel to the river. William was able to let his horses have their heads and join in the conversation.

"Even if we were not in mourning," he told his sister, "you couldn't take Ned Chivers to Gothicize at Ashwin. He has left the neighborhood on urgent private business."

"Oh dear, I hope that doesn't mean he has backed out." Lettice looked worried for a moment and then brightened up. "Perhaps he has gone to let his family know of his meaning to get married. That would be urgent private business, don't you think?"

No one was sufficiently interested to disagree.

They drove on another mile and then Hugh said, "There it is, the old house. Do you see, my love?"

Rosalba gazed across the little valley of the river to the opposite hillside, and at first she could make out nothing except trees and shadows—no great romantic mansion. Gradually she began to discern a slice of wall, a line of rooftops, halfway up the hill embowered in the woods, and soon these linked with other shapes into a hollow square, built in local stone, the tones and colors so natural to the place that it seemed to sink into its own setting and become invisible.

It was certainly very extraordinary, quite unlike the Nabob's Vineyard or Lord Retford's villa on the Thames. But the most beautiful house that Hugh had ever seen? She did not know what to say.

They had turned onto a narrow track which led them down to a narrow bridge over the river and then up again to the outer wall of Ashwin and its arched gatehouse. A carriage was drawn up there, with two liveried servants, and Mr. Sturdy was standing in the road, leaning on his strange ebony stick.

They all got out of the phaeton, which was left in the care of Mr. Sturdy's groom, and Hugh unlocked the solid, iron-studded gate with an enormous key. They moved through the archway into an open quadrangle and stared about them. The surrounding structure was of different ages and heights. The whole of the upper side was obviously Tudor with decorated stonework and three fine oriels. Flanking this, on the right, an old tower, then something that was probably a chapel, and on the left a range of plainer, more primitive buildings with a turret at either end. One huge wall was simply the remains of an old fortification. The whole place was fascinating in its way, but it should have been full of people—of the people who had lived here two hundred years ago: men-at-arms and serving wenches, thought Rosalba vaguely; strolling players and gallants in slashed doublets. Now it was silent and desolate, the desolation made more painful by the weeds that grew between the cobblestones, the self-seeded saplings and sprawling brambles that had somehow encroached into the courtyard.

Hugh scowled up at the mullioned windows. He did not speak. Some of the tiny panes were broken, and birds were nesting under the lintels.

"It's like the palace of the sleeping beauty," said Lettice.

"A melancholy sight," sighed Mr. Sturdy. "Shall we go inside?"

Hugh produced some more keys and found one to fit the front door.

Rosalba at least was pleasantly surprised by the interior, for many of the rooms were practically empty, so there were fewer signs of decay than she had expected. There were some rather shabby tapestries and a good deal of heavy oak furniture which had not come to much harm.

"Everything else was put away in my Uncle John's time," Hugh explained. "When he decided to make his home at Liston. It's not the contents that will have suffered, so much as the fabric. Good God, look at that ceiling!"

A patch of brown stain from a damp wall had spread out from the cornice to cast a blemish on an exquisite white surface of raised plasterwork. The house was full of small defects of this kind, caused by a combination of bad weather and penny-pinching neglect. The structure was sound enough; Ashwin could undoubtedly be made into a dignified (if rather remote and archaic) residence for Lady Alicia and the young baronet. Yet at this moment Hugh could think of nothing beyond the damage done to the house he had loved so much in his childhood.

Once he broke through the gloom and began to tell Rosalba about a game he and his friends had played in a small chamber at the top of the great staircase—something to do with

Cavaliers and Roundheads—but then Lettice and William and Mr. Sturdy came crowding in, and he would not go on.

It was not at all the way she had imagined seeing his beloved Ashwin.

There was one upstairs gallery, facing south, which had apparently escaped the ravages of time and desertion. It was lit by a huge window at either end, and the walls were lined with delicately carved panels of golden-gray sycamore. Here in warmth and safety a good many portraits of early Rainhams were hung, and Rosalba immediately began to look for a likeness to Hugh. She found an Elizabethan Sir Robert Rainham in gilded armor, not really like him in feature, but tall and athletic, with that formidable presence she had found so intimidating in Hugh before she came to know him properly.

"And this is Sir Robert's wife," said Mr. Sturdy at her elbow, pointing out a stiffly boned lady in a ruff the size of a cartwheel. "Mistress Mary Hall of Leicestershire. She has a most interesting pedigree. More interesting, I may say, than her descendants have so far suspected, for I have reason to think that I can trace a close connection between her and Dr. Hall of Stratford-on-Avon, who married William Shakespeare's elder daughter, Susannah."

"Indeed, sir?" said William politely.

He shot an inquiring glance at his cousin, the authority on family history. Hugh shook his head very slightly, but did not contradict the antiquarian, and Rosalba decided that Mr. Sturdy's obsession with Shakespeare was a harmless eccentricity which his friends were prepared to humor. He seemed perfectly sane in every other way.

As they passed through the next gallery, Hugh paused by an inconspicuous door in one corner.

"Where does that lead to?" Rosalba asked him.

"To the muniment room."

Hugh turned the handle and went in. She followed, not knowing what the word meant, and after her first look round she was not much the wiser. It was not a large room, and the entire floor space was taken up by ancient wooden chests. There was one stool and a small table, nothing else.

"What do they keep in here?"

"Family papers. Old documents," said Hugh absently. "That's odd."

"What is?"

Given the fact that one had so many old papers worth keeping (and such a long-established family was bound to have) there did not seem anything in the least odd about this bare and noncommittal room.

"Is anything the matter?" asked Mr. Sturdy, sticking his head round the door.

"Someone's been in here lately. Everything's been dusted."

All over the rest of the house there had been a miasma of dust, dulling every surface rising under their feet. Rosalba's fingertips were gray, and her linen dress, lawn kerchief and apron would all have to be washed. The chests in here, if not brightly polished, were surprisingly clean.

"There is not much draft," said Mr. Sturdy. "And a very small window. Less dust about, I suppose."

Hugh lifted the lid of one of the chests. It was stacked deep with bundles of paper, and there was a strong smell of mice. He let the lid drop.

"Perhaps George Robinson has been here looking for some old leases," Mr. Sturdy suggested.

"Very likely," said Hugh. "Shall we go? I think we have seen enough for one day."

As they emerged into the fresh air, Lettice said to Rosalba, "I can't help wondering whether Cousin Alicia will be comfortable in these surroundings."

"I should not care to live here myself if I was a young widow," Rosalba answered.

She had not realized that Hugh was just behind her, and wished she had kept her mouth shut.

"If that is how you feel," he said bleakly, "I hope you'll refrain from putting ideas into Alicia's head before I have had time to make the place habitable."

Rosalba felt crushed.

When they got back to Bridge Place, they found that the post from London had brought Hugh an immensely long letter from the family lawyer, who was dealing with the London end of Gus's chaotic affairs, as well as a good many letters that were probably from creditors. Hugh went off to read them.

Rosalba discovered that she had left a scarf in the orangery and went to fetch it. As she picked it up, she saw once again the figure of a man coming up from the direction of the river, and recognized Carlow's onetime crony Dan Robinson.

It was no particular surprise, for she knew, of course, that he was the brother of the agent who was mentioned so frequently in all the discussions about Ashwin. He, on the other hand, could not have known the identity of Hugh's bride, for he came to an abrupt stop and gaped at her in utter amazement.

"Mrs. Carlow!"

"No," she corrected him. "Mrs. Hugh Rainham."

Apparently this explained nothing.

"I don't understand—how can you—"

It now struck her that he would not have heard of Carlow's death. The news had reached John Meade only a short while ago.

She said, "My first husband was drowned last winter, on his way to America. You did not know?"

He shook his head.

She gave an account of Carlow's being swept overboard during a storm. He seemed stunned. Here at last, she thought, was someone who felt some grief at the news. He and Carlow had been friends, birds of a feather who had not tried to cheat each other—if only because they each knew it would be extremely difficult.

"When did you see him last?" she asked.

"Last summer," said Dan Robinson. "Just before I left France. I'd had enough of the frogs, but he was determined to stay there and make his fortune, poor fellow."

There was a short pause, then Dan Robinson added, "I'm sure I wish you happiness, Mrs. Hugh, in your changed situation."

Now that he had got over the shock, she thought he was amused by the change, which was certainly very great. He bowed and went on into the house with a portfolio that he was probably delivering for his brother.

Half an hour later, when she was sure Hugh was alone,

Rosalba ventured into the library. She found him, not in there, but in a little study at the far end which his uncle had given over to his use. He was seated at the open writing flap of a tall bureau-bookcase. He looked deathly tired.

"Is your post very troublesome, my love?" she asked sympathetically.

Hugh laid down his quill pen and said in a cold, edgy voice, "I hear you had the pleasure of informing Dan Robinson that you were now my wife. I am sure you made the most of the occasion."

"I had to explain. He had not even heard that Carlow was dead. Do you object?"

He pretended not to hear.

She guessed that Dan Robinson had annoyed him by an impudent offer of congratulations, but surely that was not enough to put him in such a bad temper? She felt she had somehow disappointed him on their tour of Ashwin, and began to praise the house, but so self-consciously that her admiration sounded stilted and insincere.

Hugh merely looked at the clock and said, "You had better go and change your dress for dinner. My uncle and aunt won't like it if you are late."

As though he too thought she did not know how to behave in a gentleman's house. In the ambiguous atmosphere of Hunsden Street he had been so certain that he wanted to marry her. Seeing her now against his own natural background, was he perhaps disillusioned, finding he had tied himself to a young woman of inferior breeding who failed to appreciate the glories of a place like Ashwin and gossiped unsuitably with the agent's scapegrace brother?

She went slowly upstairs, feeling rather forlorn and longing for the carefree happiness of the little house in Soho.

5

Dan Robinson rode up to the Bird in Hand, a posting house five miles outside Derby, on a horse he had borrowed from his brother without permission. Once inside, he asked for Mr. Chivers and was shown to a private room.

The man standing by the window turned to him eagerly.

"What's all the mystery? Why did you send for me to meet you? Has he gone?"

"Rainham? No, and not likely to. But you'll never guess what he's done."

"How should I?" with a touch of impatience.

"He's married your wife."

"He's done what?"

Edgar Carlow stared at Robinson in utter disbelief. The veneer of Ned Chivers was barely visible, nor the charm which had captivated Dorothy Lumm, which two years earlier had convinced the young Rosalba York that he was the kind of suitor she could accept. Far stronger now was the wary suspicion of the hard-pressed adventurer.

"You're hoaxing me," he said.

"No, I swear it. I've seen and spoken to her. She thinks you were drowned on your way to America."

"I wonder who gave her that idea. Or how she came to be on such terms with Rainham. Not that it matters, for don't you see what this means, Dan? I've got them in my power. That prudish little icicle is a bigamist—a common criminal—and Mr. high-and-mighty Rainham will have to pay through the nose if he wants me to keep quiet."

"She didn't look like an icicle to me," said Dan slyly. "She's handsomer than ever."

Carlow scowled. He did not welcome the hint that Rosalba's frigidity had been due to a contemptuous dislike of himself. Then he began to laugh.

"To think I'd given up any hope of making money out of the girl. It's like being dealt an ace when you thought there were none left in the pack."

"Yes, I can see the attraction," said Robinson. "There's only one snag. If you persuade Rainham to buy you off, how can you come back to Trilbourne and pay your addresses to Dorothy Lumm?"

"Why, easily!" said Carlow after a slight check. "They won't be able to interfere. They can't expose my first marriage without getting themselves caught in the same net. They'll never do that."

"I'm not so sure. Listen to me, Ned: I've had more time to think this over than you have." Robinson sat down in a large Windsor chair, propping his feet on the empty hearth and absently scrutinizing a set of Hogarth prints depicting *The Rake's Progress*, while he sorted out the thoughts that had been seething in his mind ever since he had seen Rosalba in the orangery at Bridge Place.

"Hugh Rainham's a high-minded paragon—that's why he and Gus could never see eye to eye—and you've always said the girl spoiled half your schemes by being so foolishly scrupulous. Granted, such people dearly love to be respectable, and I daresay they might pay you to go away and leave them in peace, but do you think they'll be content to sit back and say nothing while you deceive Miss Moneybags with a false marriage? It's not as though your wife stands in much danger of being prosecuted, for I reckon she must have been misinformed about some other fellow who was lost at sea, and no court would convict her. On the other hand, if you marry the heiress while your first wife is living in the same town, you will run the risk of transportation. In fact, it is Hugh Rainham who'll be in a position to threaten you."

"And if he doesn't, you will," remarked Carlow with a sour grimace. "I thank you for the warning."

"My dear Ned, what a shocking suggestion!"

Robinson was amused rather than insulted, though he was glad to find that his dark predictions had frightened Carlow off his idea of trying to extort money from the redoubtable Hugh Rainham. Dan thought this a very chancy undertaking in which he had no wish to become involved—and involved he would be, as a person who had known all along the real identity of Mr. Chivers. Of course it now seemed an act of lunacy ever to have brought Carlow to Trilbourne. But a month ago everything seemed to be propitious, besides being perfectly safe.

Dan Robinson had been speaking the truth when he told Rosalba that he had left Carlow in France. After some further adventures Carlow had come back to England practically penniless. He had made the usual appeal to his family, who had decided to get rid of him by paying his passage to America. On landing in the colony, the ship's captain was to hand over to him a sum of money to start him off in the New World. Carlow did not want to go to America. However, he boarded the *Pocahontas* at Deptford and speedily persuaded the captain that if the money was produced at once they could share it between them. So the ship sailed without her unwilling passenger, and Carlow assumed a new name and went northwards to try his luck in York. He had been getting on quite prosperously when a quarrel over a game of cards led to a duel and he had been obliged to leave the city in a hurry. Thrown out of his calculations and uncertain what to do next, he had written a cautious letter to Dan Robinson, who could generally be reached through his family in Trilbourne.

The reply had come instantly. Dan was actually in Trilbourne himself and he had just devised a wonderful scheme for making money—a scheme in which Ned would be of the greatest assistance. Ned might hesitate before coming to Trilbourne, the Rainham stronghold, but he could rest assured that neither Gus nor Hugh ever set foot in the place and they were the only members of the family who knew him by sight. So Carlow had come to Trilbourne in his new persona as Mr. Edward Chivers, a young man of fortune who was thinking of settling in the district. Dan's scheme was turning out even better than they expected when a new and glorious prospect came into view. After years of trying unsuccessfully to marry for money, Carlow had at last met an heiress who was not only ready to fall into his arms but was also totally free from interfering relations.

It was almost too good to be true. Mrs. Lumm was a kind, silly woman, quite under her daughter's thumb, and because of the inequality of the parents' marriage (she poor and genteel, he rich and vulgar) they had cut themselves off from both families. Dorothy was twenty-one and her own mistress.

The distant firm of attorneys in Birmingham need not be notified until after the marriage, when it would be too late for them to tie up the bride's fortune in some exasperating settlement. The fact that he was already married had scarcely crossed Carlow's mind, for he never expected to hear of Rosalba again.

And now, by the sheer perversity of fate, she had turned up in Trilbourne to prevent him from making this far more satisfactory match. For he had to admit that Dan was right. Rosalba would never allow him to go through a false marriage with another woman. She'd say it was her duty to save the poor creature, even if she was acting out of pure spite.

"What do you want me to do?" he asked sulkily. "Get what I can out of Rainham and then vanish?"

"I have a better notion. You should leave Rainham alone, forget any vengeful feelings toward Rosalba, and concentrate on courting and marrying Dorothy Lumm."

"How can I? You said yourself it would be impossible while those two remain in Trilbourne."

"I've thought of a plan. It so happens that an acquaintance of my brother George's has been instructed to sell a West Indian sugar plantation. What you have to do is this. First of all, you put down an advance payment as earnest of your good faith. Then you return to Trilbourne and tell Miss Lumm that you have inherited a plantation in Jamaica and must go out there immediately; you wish to marry her at once so that she can accompany you. I don't think she'll make difficulties. The moment the ring is on her finger, you will have control of her fortune and you can complete the purchase of the estate. You set sail for the Indies together; I daresay it may prove a very pleasant interlude, living in a fine house surrounded by every luxury that the tropic region affords and waited on by an army of slaves. You may even wish to stay there."

Carlow had been showing signs of dissent ever since the mention of a down payment, but Robinson gave him no chance to interrupt.

"If you wish to come home after a year or so, you simply tell your wife that you would prefer to settle in a county other than Derbyshire. With reasonable care you need never run across the Rainhams again."

"It would be simpler still," said Carlow thoughtfully, "to leave my wife in the West Indies while I came home on business connected with her property in England. Once I had turned everything into cash, I could afford to dispense with Ned Chivers, and Ned Carlow could then reappear, having made his fortune in America. No fear of a prosecution for bigamy, no tedious provincial wife—I could be rid of both and live very well on the proceeds."

There was a note of triumph in his voice. Robinson laughed, a little uncomfortably. He was not so cold-hearted as his friend.

"I can find only two obstacles," added Carlow. "Where am I to raise the money to secure a first refusal of the plantation? And how the devil am I to fix my interest with Dorothy while she is in Trilbourne? I daren't go near the place."

"You can if you act quickly. The Rainhams are all in deep mourning for the late lamented baronet; they won't attend any social gatherings at present. You can safely visit the Lumms, sweep the fair Dorothy off her feet, and persuade her mother the wedding must take place quietly in London."

"On account of our departure for Jamaica and all the necessary preparations. Yes, that would serve. I rather fancy myself as the master of a sugar plantation. But the money for the original outlay—how am I to get hold of that?"

"Why, from our other golden goose," said Robinson, smiling. "We can raise our prices a little. He won't quibble. And I'll lend you my share."

Carlow became wary. "What do you expect to gain from this?"

"Your bond for three thousand pounds, payable the day after your marriage to Dorothy Lumm."

"Three thousand! That's a trifle steep."

"Her fortune is five times as great."

Carlow haggled as a matter of principle, but soon gave in. He knew he could not succeed without his accomplice. He sent for a bottle of wine and they toasted each other, and drank cynically to the bride, whose happiness was not likely to last very long.

"I must go," said Robinson, when various details had been discussed and the bottle was empty.

"You've forgotten something. I thought you wanted a further sample."

"Have you one ready? Let me see."

Carlow took from his pocket a folded piece of paper which looked about a hundred years old (as indeed it was, having been carefully cut from the last, blank sheet of an old inventory). It was now written over with curiously spiky writing in brownish ink. He handed this to Robinson, who deciphered a few lines with difficulty and read them aloud:

> "... 'My good lord Merlin,
> If you have writ your annals true, this there,
> That like an eagle in a dovecot, I
> Fluttered the infidels at Baden...'

Fine incomprehensible stuff. You have a talent."

Carlow smirked and said he was flattered.

6

"I don't know what I should do without Hugh," said Alicia.

She and Rosalba were sitting in the open doorway of the orangery, watching the nursemaid as she walked up and down the lawn, giving the infant baronet his airing. Rosalba thought with longing of her baby Anne, far away in Islington, and wondered when she would see her again. Alicia went on expressing her grateful admiration of Hugh.

"He is so wise and so patient, and always dependable, like a rock. As well as being very kind. To have a man one can rely on, after poor Gus—well, I know I should not say this, but there was not a day in my married life that I was not frightened of what he would do and what would happen next. And hardly a night that I did not cry myself to sleep."

Rosalba listened with sympathy, thinking that Gus must have made an even worse husband than Carlow.

"Was he always unkind to you, right from the start?"

"He did not mean to be, not at first. Only he was so weak, and so silly when he got drunk—and he was drunk very often, you know, for wine and spirits went straight to his head, which was not his fault, poor fellow. And when he was the worse for drink, I—I could not hide my repugnance, which made him angry, so that he turned against me and liked to torment me. I should never have married him, for I knew even then that he was not quite steady. But I had all sorts of foolish, heroic ideas of reforming him. And Papa was so anxious for the match."

Rosalba knew that Lord Petersfield was a poor man. At least he was a poor earl, and though this was not quite the same thing, it meant that he had no money to settle on his daughters, so it was not at all easy to find them husbands of suitable rank.

"If my sister Mary had lived," continued Alicia, "there would have been an alliance between our family and the Rainhams. It was all arranged, and then Mary caught the smallpox and died. We had none of us had the inoculation; Papa thought it would be irreligious to thwart the will of Providence."

The more Rosalba heard about Lord Petersfield, the less she liked him.

"Your sister was engaged to Gus?"

"Oh no," replied Alicia in gentle surprise. "Mary was engaged to Hugh. I thought you must have known."

Rosalba had not known. She had sometimes wondered how such an attractive man with a private fortune had managed to stay single so long. Now this was explained, as Alicia spoke of her childish memories of Hugh, handsome as a romantic knight in a tale of chivalry, coming to court her eldest sister. All this was said quite innocently, without any intention of causing pain. She's half in love with him herself, thought Hugh's wife.

As Alicia went on talking about Hugh's great thoughtfulness and care for herself and little Theo, it struck Rosalba that he was certainly showing more interest in them than he showed in her at present.

It was extraordinary and rather frightening how distant and different he had become since their arrival in Derbyshire.

133

Of course he was preoccupied and overburdened with work, trying to unravel the disastrous state of affairs left by Gus, who, knowing he could not sell an acre of the Ashwin estate, had bled it dry for the last three years. So Rosalba saw very little of her new husband and they were seldom alone, in a house full of his relations. Even at night, being married to Hugh was not what she had expected. They had been given a handsome bedchamber and a wide matrimonial bed; there was a dressing room next door with a sofa bed against the wall. Rosalba saw this at first as one of the impressive if unnecessary luxuries of her new life (like the smart young maid whose sole employment was to act as her dresser and look after her clothes). But at Bridge Place the men always sat up later than the ladies; Hugh and his uncle had long solemn conferences, and when he did come to bed, more often than not he slept in the dressing room. Rosalba was hurt and bewildered, the more so because she did not really know— and could not bring herself to ask—whether this behavior was as odd as it seemed to her, or whether it was quite natural in the state of life to which she had been raised. People of consequence had these extra beds, so presumably they used them. But surely not so early in a marriage? Or did Hugh feel that a year and a half of rapture in Hunsden Street had given them licence enough, and that it was high time they settled down to be domesticated and genteel?

He was so critical of her nowadays.

"Why do you wander about by yourself?" he asked her once when she had come to look for him in the library. "Have you nothing better to do? It looks so odd."

"It's not my fault. I have no occupation here and your family don't want me."

"That's nonsense, Rosalba. They have all done their best to make you feel at home. Except Olivia, I'm afraid, but she will soon be returning to town. I suppose you are discontented because you are forced to rusticate here instead of touring on the Continent. It's just one of the inconveniences of family life that one so often has to put duty before pleasure. If you had thought of that perhaps you would not have been so anxious to marry me."

"What do you mean—anxious?"

"Well, weren't you?" he replied with a challenging glance. Rosalba turned and walked out of the library. She went upstairs and shut herself in their room. What a cruel thing for him to say: as though she had trapped him.

Well, perhaps she had, without meaning to. By crying and being fragile after Anne was born. By her unconcealed remorse when the clergyman had admonished her so severely at the christening; and then by jumping at the offer Hugh had probably felt in honor bound to make to her, the moment he heard she was free.

Presently she went downstairs again. Glancing through the half-open door of the library while she summoned the courage to go in, she saw that Hugh was now deep in a conference with Alicia; they were studying an estate map, while Theo played at their feet. He seemed to be fascinated by his large cousin's boots. Hugh looked down, picked up the little boy and hoisted him onto his shoulder.

How domesticated they seem, thought Rosalba enviously. A new thought pierced her like an arrow: suppose Hugh was falling in love with Alicia?

It was not impossible. He had always shown a special concern for her; she was the younger sister of the girl he had once hoped to marry and perhaps very like her. During the lifetime of her deplorable husband, Alicia had been at a disadvantage—timid and withdrawn, too virtuous to encourage other men, and probably too disgusted by the treatment she had to put up with from Gus. Yet she was charming in her gentle way, and there was no longer anyone for her to be frightened of. She might never feel or inspire an overmastering passion, but would that in itself be a recommendation to Hugh? Did he really want a wife who behaved in bed with the sensuous abandon he had taught Rosalba in Hunsden Street? He had not made love to her in that way since they came to Derbyshire.

If Hugh had been able to marry his cousin's widow, they could have lived together at Ashwin and he could have been a father to young Theo, better placed than anyone to save him from the follies that had killed his real father. Instead Hugh had married Rosalba. Gus was already dead on the morning of their wedding, and Alicia a widow, but they had not known it.

She could hear Hugh describing to Alicia the old nurseries at Ashwin. Miserably she crept away.

That night Hugh came to their room and tried to close the gap that was growing between them.

"I am sorry you are not happy here," he said. "Perhaps I should have left you in town—though I suppose that would not have suited you either. It is a pity you have never learned to trust me."

What could he mean? Did he suspect that she might become jealous of Alicia?

She gazed at him in mute entreaty.

He did not explain, but lay down beside her and began to make love to her, imperiously and with all the uncensored passion of Soho. Yet something was wrong. Although she responded eagerly, craving for affection and reassurance, she ended with a sense of exhausted isolation. They were like two riders galloping towards each other without ever meeting.

They lay still, staring up into the silk-lined canopy.

"My poor girl," he said gently, running his fingertips over the creamy skin of her shoulder.

Rosalba prickled up instantly. She was not going to be treated as an object of compassion, someone he had to pet and caress out of pity, or worse still, duty. She rolled over to the far side of the bed, fording a yawn and saying, "Do let me go to sleep."

The next night he was back in the dressing room.

When the funeral took place it was probably the most dignified event of Gus Rainham's career, attended by his male relatives and many of his neighbors and tenants. Of course no ladies were present.

Olivia now returned to London. This was an admission of defeat; she had failed to persuade any of the family to cold-shoulder Hugh's unsuitable wife. Rosalba should have been triumphant, but she was too unhappy to care. She wandered about Bridge Place, longing for the little house in Hunsden Street; it seemed extraordinary that a few weeks ago she had felt herself a prisoner there. She was like a bird that had escaped from a cage, only to find itself unfit to survive in a tree.

Sometimes she followed the path that led down to the riverbank and along as far as the new bridge (so called to distinguish it from the ancient crossing over the Tirrel close by Bridge Place). Although this reach of the river ran along one side of the town, it was pretty and secluded, for the fine houses in the High Street had long narrow gardens stretching down towards the water and the only buildings visible from the footpath were the upper stories of these houses seen through a curtain of lacy branches. There was just one house at the water's edge, formerly occupied by a ferryman. The ferry had fallen into disuse after the new bridge was built, and the cottage stood empty, looking picturesque at a distance and derelict when you got near. On the opposite side of the river there were some rustic dwellings, an orchard, and a sawmill with its tributary stream, but the inhabitants of this little colony did not seem very numerous or very busy, apart from the bees that flew in and out of the straw skeps under the apple trees.

Rosalba was idling along the riverbank one afternoon when she saw a man coming towards her. She retreated behind the wall of the ferryman's cottage, for she was in such low spirits that she did not want to meet even a casual passerby. And this was not an artisan or laborer; by his dress he was a gentleman, and there was something about him, his outline and the way he moved, that seemed familiar, even though he was too far off for her to make out his features. He came on towards her, his head and face still masked by the thick shadow of some overhanging trees. Then he emerged into the sunlight, glanced round him, and turned into an alley that ran between two of the gardens.

She saw him for the briefest glimpse, but it was enough to give her the most violent shock. She was sure—she was almost sure—that he was her first husband, Edgar Carlow.

But he's dead, she told herself. She started to run towards the turning he had taken, and then stopped, realizing that she didn't want to see Carlow—if it was Carlow—and still less did she want him to see her. She leaned against the cottage rail, feeling for the second time in her life as though she was going to faint. I'm going out of my mind, she thought. Seeing things. How could it be Carlow, who was drowned in a storm at sea? Yet the image of that man's face was engraved on her memory with the bite of acid on a copper plate; she had lived with him for five months, and in the common phrase she would have known him anywhere.

Instinctively she started back along the path to the safety of Bridge Place. What was she to do? Let Hugh know that she imagined she had seen the ghost of her dead husband? For that was what it would sound like. Or that she had exaggerated a chance resemblance into a recognition that was absurd and hysterical? In his present mood Hugh would be irritated and scornful. Worse still, he might even hope that Carlow was still alive, for in that case, it now dawned on her, their own marriage would be invalid. To see such a thought in his eyes was something she could not endure. So it was impossible to confide in Hugh.

When she reached the house, she found the females of the family fussing round little Theo, who had a rash and a slight fever. He was probably cutting a tooth. Rosalba was grateful for the diversion, which meant that no one had time to notice her condition of nervous anxiety. When she went to bed, she had the room to herself once again, so she was free to lie awake and worry.

How reliable was the information about Carlow's death? Everything seemed to hang on that. Was there anyone who could say positively that he really had been drowned in the storm? The one person who might help her to discover this was John Meade. She would write to him in the morning and ask if there could have been a mistake. If not, if Carlow had definitely been drowned, then the man on the footpath must have been a stranger who looked very like him. Such astonishing coincidences were not impossible.

7

Rosalba wrote her letter to John Meade, and William Rainham arranged to have it posted. He was an impressionable young man and accepted it as quite natural that his cousin's wife should correspond with her first husband's attorney.

As soon as she had taken an active step to dispel her fears, Rosalba began to feel a great deal more cheerful. The belief that she had seen Carlow on the riverbank faded during the next week. Of course it was a delusion; she could not think why she had been so silly.

And then, one morning when she and Alicia were coming in from the garden, they met Dan Robinson crossing the hall; once again he was acting as a messenger for his brother, the land agent.

He bowed respectfully to the mother of the young baronet, and more slightly to Rosalba, managing to look her straight in the eye.

"Good morning, *Mrs. Hugh.*"

The way he spoke her new name—as though he knew she was not entitled to use it—destroyed all her recovered complacency, for she realized at once that he was and always had been the link between Carlow and the Rainhams. He must have known all along that Carlow was alive; that was why he had been so astounded when she told him she was married to Hugh. After which he had personally summoned his friend to Trilbourne, to make the most of a promising situation.

"Are you not feeling well?" Alicia asked her.

Rosalba said something about the heat; she had no idea how white she had gone.

Alicia decided that Rosalba might be pregnant again (she knew about little Anne, put out to nurse in Islington). Rosalba's situation was still rather ambiguous; it was too soon for the family to forget that her first child had been born out of wedlock, and perhaps she did not wish to draw attention to herself.

They were going over to Ashwin in half an hour, the whole

family party, to see what the carpenters and masons were doing in the house. Rosalba cried off, pleading a headache which was quite genuine. She could tell that Hugh was put out, more annoyed than disappointed probably. She could not help that.

She went and sat in her room, made so stupid with dread that it was impossible to think or plan. There Nemesis overtook her in the early afternoon, when one of the footmen came to announce that a gentleman had called to see her. So here was Carlow at last, demanding his pound of flesh.

"To see me? Are you sure?"

"Yes, Mrs. Hugh. I've put him in the library, though he didn't give his name. Shall I say you are not at home?"

"No, I'll see what he wants."

She got up slowly, with a sense of inevitability, and went downstairs. She felt sick at the thought of the coming interview. She did not know what she was going to do or say. She supposed Carlow would ask for money. She had not got any money. If he tried to attack her, she could call the servants, and then there would be a scandal. Bracing her courage, she went into the library. The man standing near the fireplace was slighter and darker than Carlow. For a moment she did not recognize him. Then he started forward, and she saw it was John Meade.

"Oh, it's you!" she exclaimed, smiling so warmly that he felt certain of his welcome and kissed her hand with barely concealed ardor.

Rosalba remembered that Mr. Meade needed very little encouragement, so she withdrew a little, saying conventionally, "How kind of you to come and see me. Won't you sit down? I'm afraid I may have troubled you for a reassurance you will not be able to give me, for I am now convinced that Carlow is alive and in Trilbourne."

"I suppose you never received my letter?"

John Meade spoke in a low, tense voice, and she noticed now that he was extremely ill at ease.

"What letter?"

"The one I addressed to you in Hunsden Street, shortly after you informed me of your intention to marry Rainham. I suppose it must have gone astray."

She remembered now: the long screed had been delivered on her wedding day, and she had pushed it aside, not wanting to waste time over what she took to be a tedious declaration of unrequited love when she was on the point of leaving for the church. But perhaps the length of the letter had been due to something entirely different.

"There was a mistake," she said, with a sense of doom. "You were writing to warn me that my husband was still living."

He made a slight gesture of assent.

"Oh God, was ever anything so unlucky! But how did such a confusion come about? Who was the man that was swept overboard in the storm?"

"No one was swept overboard. There was no storm," he said despairingly.

Rosalba was baffled. "I don't understand. Why should the captain have told such a tale?"

"It wasn't the captain. I heard nothing from the captain. I made up the whole account myself."

"*Made it up?* You cannot be serious."

Meade sat hunched in his chair, clenching and unclenching his fingers in a knot of unbearable strain.

"It was after Edgar set sail for America—"

"But he isn't in America," interrupted Rosalba. "He is here in Trilbourne, I tell you! I saw him within the last week."

She was beginning to wonder whether the sensible young lawyer was going off his head.

"He was supposed to go to America—that was made a condition when his brother paid up yet again and saved him from being charged with forgery, not for the first time. How he contrived to stay in England and what he lived on I don't know. I saw him aboard the ship myself, the day before she sailed."

Meade fell silent for a moment, gazing dully at the rows of books on the open shelves, as though they might supply him with some inspiration to continue his story. Then he went doggedly on.

"I visited you in Soho, soon after your daughter was born. I could see you were very unhappy, that your irregular life, your ambiguous position, made it impossible for you to find peace of mind. It struck me forcibly that nothing except Edgar

141

Carlow's death could set you free to form a more stable connection, and that once he set foot on that great continent, he would be lost from view—in fact, that was what his brother was hoping for—so that even if he was to die, you would never hear of it. You would be tied to a family skeleton for the rest of your life. And I thought suddenly that if I told you he was dead, you would be able to marry again in good faith and without a qualm of conscience. I was ready to bear the weight of any sin that was committed, I meant to cherish and protect you—"

"Surely you never imagined I should accept such an offer!" exclaimed Rosalba, and the note of angry incredulity must have been a stinging punishment for his presumption. "You knew I was in love with Hugh Rainham."

"I did not think he would marry you."

And he probably wishes he hadn't, thought Rosalba, though she was not going to give this away. At least Hugh's loyalty and affection had been strong and spontaneous, even if he had regretted this later.

"When I heard of your intended marriage, I came to my senses. I wrote to warn you—"

"I wonder why. If you wanted me to live happily in a fool's paradise, you might have let me live there with Hugh."

He gazed at her with the miserable eyes of a beaten dog.

"I know I have done you a fearful injury. Once I heard the wedding had taken place, I resolved to keep my mouth shut and hope for the best. I never supposed that Edgar was still in England. If you will tell me how I can help you, try to make amends—"

"What can anyone do?" she retorted impatiently. "Thanks to your interference and folly, I shall either be accused of bigamy or I shall have to be ransomed by the payment of enormous sums of money which Carlow will demand for his silence."

She got up with a movement of restless irritation and went over to the window, turning her back on the library. On the lawn outside a man was swinging a scythe while another came behind him with a rake to comb away the shorn grass. She watched these activities with a kind of dumb incomprehension as though she had never seen anything like them before.

"Mrs. Rainham."

Rosalba almost said, "I am not Mrs. Rainham," but held back the bitter reminder because she knew she had the power to hurt John Meade too much, simply because he loved her. She had become sensitive to this dangerous power during the last two weeks.

"I have been wondering," he said, "whether I could make some sort of reparation by sending Carlow away."

She was not impressed. "How do you propose to do that?"

"I know too much about him for his own comfort. A word in the right place and I can have him put under lock and key."

"But then he'll make a scandal about my second marriage, if only out of spite."

"No, he won't. Consider for a moment. You and Rainham are at a disadvantage, because he has a hold over you. I, on the other hand, am his brother's representative, and he will be somewhat embarrassed to meet me in Derbyshire after he was paid to go to America. I can threaten him, but he will not threaten me, for he can have no idea that there is a weapon ready to his hand. As far as he is aware, you and I have never met, save on the one occasion when you both visited my chambers two years ago. He must assume that your fate is a matter of complete indifference to me, so he won't try to strike a bargain. He'll leave the country this time, I'll see to that. And he'll have no opportunities to stir up trouble."

"Are you sure?"

John Meade had recovered some confidence with his lawyerlike manner.

"Leave it to me. Henry Carlow has been very patient until now—no man cares to inform on his own brother—but if I tell Master Edgar that his family's forbearance has now expired, he'll believe me. At least he will not run the risk of disbelieving me. I shall pretend, you see, that we got news of his being still in England, and that I have traveled up to Derbyshire in pursuit of him. That should provide the necessary shock to his nerves. But first I must find him. He is not at the Sun in Splendor, for I made discreet inquiries when I arrived there."

"He may be using an assumed name."

"Very likely, but there is no such person at the inn."

"I expect you will be able to trace him through his crony Dan Robinson. I'm convinced it was he who brought Carlow here when he discovered that Hugh and I were married."

In any case it ought not to be difficult to find a stranger of Carlow's type in a little town like Trilbourne.

"He is hardly one to pass unnoticed," commented Meade. "So I'll be on my way. Shall I come and see you again when I have some news?"

Rosalba hesitated. She was no longer angry with him. But she did not want him haunting Bridge Place; the Rainhams would think it strange, and it was unusual for them all to be out, as they were today.

John Meade saw her reluctance and perhaps misinterpreted it.

"You want to see the back of me, and I don't blame you. I cannot tell you how sorry I am for all the distress I have caused. The agonies of apprehension. Well, you need fear nothing more. I'll get rid of that scoundrel, I promise you."

A moment later he was gone.

8

"I should like to take you to call on Mrs. Lumm," Hugh said to Rosalba. "Unless perhaps you have another headache?"

The cool voice and the ironic glance made her uncomfortable.

"Of course not—I don't know why you should suppose— that is, I shall be very glad to come with you."

It was Saturday. John Meade had visited her on Thursday, and on the intervening Friday Rosalba had stayed indoors and the only outsiders seen at Bridge Place had been the apothecary with a soothing wash for Sir Theodore's swollen gums, and Miss Dorothy Lumm, who came to talk interminably to Lettice about her wedding.

So Rosalba had no means of knowing whether Meade had been able to meet Carlow and frighten him away from Derbyshire. She would have felt safer if she could have waited a day or two longer, but with Hugh making skeptical remarks about headaches, that was impossible.

The etiquette of mourning had prevented her from receiving and returning the calls due to Hugh's bride and she had hardly set foot in the town, which had probably saved her from coming face to face with Carlow. She had been to church, of course, but she had not expected to see him there, nor had she done so.

She took Hugh's arm and gazed about her apprehensively as they emerged from the grounds of Bridge Place into the broad High Street.

"I did not think it worth ordering the carriage for so short a distance," he said. "You don't mind walking, do you?"

"Not in the least."

There were not many people about. Hugh said this was because it was market day; there would be a crowd concentrated at the commercial end of the town, near the new bridge. He seemed to know most of the passersby, and they gazed at Rosalba with a respectful interest.

"You are not nervous of appearing in public?" he asked her, clearly able to sense some kind of anxiety through the pressure of her fingers on his arm. "You need not be. This is a provincial backwater, and there is no one here to alarm you."

Rosalba smiled and said she was not at all nervous.

He thought she was afraid of being snubbed or despised by anyone who knew her past history, and was trying gently to reassure her. He was being so kind, and she felt the most deceitful wretch she wanted to burst into tears.

To divert his attention, she asked about the buildings on the right side of the street.

"Are those the houses you can see through the trees from the riverbank?"

"Yes. That one over there, with the high steps and the pierced fanlight, belongs to Mr. Sturdy."

There was a narrow gap between Mr. Sturdy's house and the one next to it; Rosalba was wondering whether this was the same alley or lane that Carlow had turned into from the river path, when a top-heavy, brightly painted coach lumbered past them.

"The northbound stage," remarked Hugh. "They change horses at the Sun in Splendor further along the street."

Mention of the posting inn reminded her of Meade; was he still in Trilbourne? Were they in danger of meeting him as well as Carlow? That too would be awkward in a lesser degree, difficult to explain.

She must have made an involuntary check, for Hugh asked her what was the matter, and she had to pretend she had twisted her ankle. She was thankful to arrive at the Lumms' house, which was on their left, the side of the High Street furthest from the river.

They were shown into an upstairs drawing room, where their hostess was sitting alone: a still-pretty woman in her forties with an elegant taste in ruffles and laces.

"This is delightful," she exclaimed. "I do congratulate you, my dear Hugh. I should have called on your wife long before this, but it seems unfeeling to be paying bridal visits in a house where there is such a very recent widow."

"That is what we thought, so I have broken all the rules and brought Rosalba to you instead."

Mrs. Lumm was about twelve years older than Hugh and had known him since he was a small child, so she still used his Christian name. They began to converse easily. Rosalba was quite glad to sit passive, listening to them, in this very feminine room. The walls were hung with silk the color of crushed strawberries; the frieze and cornice were decorated with plaster garlands that stood out like whipped cream.

"And I hear Dorothy is going to be married," said Hugh. "I hope you are pleased with the young man. He comes from the West Indies, I believe?"

"I like him excessively, he is everything one could wish. But he does not come from the West Indies."

"Well, I did not suppose him to be a blackamoor!"

"He is not even a white Jamaican," she said, laughing. "He is going out there and taking Dorothy with him—that is why they are anxious to hurry on the marriage—because he has never seen this plantation he has inherited, and he wants her at his side. To see whether they can bear to live

146

there, at least for a year or so, while they are setting things to rights. Of course she is mad to go, and I cannot think it would be right for me to complain and make difficulties, though I shall miss her sadly."

Mrs. Lumm burbled happily on, saying how lucky Dorothy had been to captivate such a suitor, and in Trilbourne of all places. If his uncle had died a few weeks earlier, it would never have happened, for Ned had arrived in Derbyshire intending to buy an estate, had consulted George Robinson and had thus been introduced into local society; he had danced with Dorothy at one of the assemblies. Then his uncle had left him the sugar plantation, but by now the young people were in love and determined to marry.

"Have you met his family?" asked Hugh.

"Poor boy, he has no family. No one close, at all events. Oh, I see how it is: you think I should make all sorts of inquiries about his origins and his ancestors. Gentlemen are always such sticklers! I can assure you that Edward Chivers is a most respectable person. Mr. Sturdy approves of him, and you know how particular he is where Dorothy is concerned, she is such a pet of his."

As she listened, Rosalba was struck by a horrible possibility. As a newcomer to Trilbourne, hearing endless chat about neighbors who were mere names to her, she had imagined that Lettice's friend the heiress was engaged to someone they all knew, a member of a well-known family who had made their money out of sugar. She had taken very little interest in Lettice's eulogies about Dorothy's handsome lover, being too preoccupied with her own affairs. Only now she realized that this plausible charmer, with his fortune and his plantation that no one had actually vouched for, had created much the same good impression as Carlow when he descended on the Suffolk village, intent on marrying the squire's sister. He had failed, because the squire had seen through him. But if Edgar Carlow had transformed himself into Edward Chivers (good heavens, they even had the same initials) his latest heiress had a much less perceptive guardian. She and her mother were likely to become the victims of a most cruel fraud. I must find out for certain, thought Rosalba.

"I hear your future son-in-law is a very fine young man,"

she said rather too effusively, hoping to prompt a description. "I'm sure all the young ladies in Trilbourne must be green with envy."

It was a silly, vulgar way of talking which drew a puzzled glance from Hugh. Mrs. Lumm did not appear to mind. She opened a portfolio that was lying on the harpsichord and took out a sheet of paper which she handed to Rosalba.

"Dorothy made this little portrait of him; I want to have it framed."

It was a pencil sketch, lightly touched in with water color. Dorothy Lumm had only a very moderate talent, but she had been carefully taught, and the slim, fair-haired paragon posed heroically beside an unlikely Doric pillar was a recognizable image of Carlow.

Rosalba murmured something civil and laid down the sketch on a nearby table instead of passing it to Hugh, as Mrs. Lumm probably expected. Luckily he did not ask for it, having no great interest in pictures of perfect strangers by their besotted admirers.

Oh God, what am I to do? wondered Rosalba in agonies of indecision. I shall have to speak out now; I can't let Carlow ruin the wretched girl's happiness and go off with all her money. I must tell Hugh the minute we are alone, and he will deal with everything.

Then it seemed as though she was going to lose that chance of warning him in private, for there were quick footsteps on the stairs; someone was hurrying up to the drawing room.

"Here is Dorothy," said Mrs. Lumm. "And bringing Ned with her, I don't doubt. We expected him to spend yesterday evening with us, and when he did not arrive, we were a little afraid that he might not be well—he is not very strong. However, she sounds so eager that I'm sure he must be with her now."

Rosalba sat petrified in her chair, feeling as though her rib cage was contracting so that she could hardly breathe.

The door swung open and Dorothy Lumm came bounding in, pink and breathless.

"Mama, what are we to do? Ned is not in at Mrs. Copley's—"

"I expect he has gone for an early ride," said Mrs. Lumm

148

placidly. "At least he cannot be ill. But what are you thinking of, my love! Do you not see that Mr. and Mrs. Hugh Rainham have come to call on us?"

"I beg your pardon, Mrs. Rainham—how do you do?" Dorothy made Rosalba a polite if absent-minded curtsy and turned back to her mother.

"You don't understand, Mama. Ned didn't go out this morning, he went out yesterday afternoon and never came back. Mrs. Copley is so alarmed that she has been making inquiries in the town, but no one has seen him. He has completely disappeared."

9

"But what can have happened to him?" asked Dorothy for about the sixth time.

And they had to go into the circumstances all over again. The so-called Mr. Chivers had rooms in the house of a Mrs. Copley, a very worthy widow, on the outskirts of the town beyond Market Place. He had dined at his lodging and gone out shortly after four o'clock, without saying where he was going—though she had assumed that he would be calling on Miss Lumm, for their engagement was known and much discussed in Trilbourne. It was true the Lumms expected him, but not much before seven; he had promised to drink tea with them and spend the evening. So where was he going when he left his lodging with several hours to spare?

"How was he dressed?" asked Hugh.

"In breeches and stockings, Mrs. Copley says, and his blue coat. Not in boots, so he cannot have gone for a ride, if that is what you are thinking, Mr. Rainham. Though he does keep a horse at the livery."

"Might he have taken a stroll into the country and lost his way?" suggested Hugh. "If so, he will have spent the night at some cottage or farmhouse, and he will soon be back in Trilbourne, feeling rather foolish, I dare say."

He was doing his best to calm the two agitated ladies.

Rosalba could do nothing but look sympathetic, though her mind was working furiously.

"Suppose he met with an accident?" said Dorothy with a break in her voice. "He may have been lying out all night with a broken leg!"

"There is no call to imagine anything so dreadful, my love," said her mother. "Though I do think that he may have walked too far for his strength and perhaps been obliged to seek shelter for the night, for I have thought him a little out of sorts in the last fortnight. Not always wanting to be out and about, as he was when we first met him."

"That is because he wants to keep me to himself," said Dorothy, complacent in spite of her anxiety.

You're wrong there, thought Rosalba. It was because he was afraid of meeting me. She had realized by now that Carlow had not come here to extort money from Hugh; he had been in Trilbourne already (invited by that rogue Dan Robinson, of course) and chasing an heiress. The very last person he wanted to see was his lawful wife, and while she had been dreading a visit from him, he had been more or less hiding from her.

"If there is anything we can do to help, you have only to ask," Hugh was saying.

He signed to Rosalba that it was time for them to leave.

They made their farewells, both assuring poor Dorothy that she would soon have good news and would be able to laugh at her fears. Rosalba felt the most complete hypocrite.

For the explanation of Carlow's disappearance dawned on her as she walked sedately down the wide staircase at Hugh's side. John Meade had put him to flight.

In the hall they encountered Mr. Sturdy, who had just heard the news and was coming to offer comfort and advice.

"I'm sure they will be glad to see you, sir," said Hugh. "At present they are inclined to make mountains out of molehills—at least I hope they are molehills. What kind of a fellow is Chivers?"

"A most excellent young man," said Mr. Sturdy. "I took to him from the start—in fact, I believe I presented him to little Dolly at one of our balls. Poor girl, I hope nothing has occurred to cause her any real distress."

The old magistrate looked painfully distressed himself at the mere idea.

"Chivers," remarked Hugh thoughtfully. "I don't recall hearing the name."

"Well, perhaps not. It is a recent fortune, I believe. Sugar. But he'd pass anywhere. He certainly has the manner and breeding of a gentleman."

In this old Mr. Sturdy was perfectly right. Rosalba could tell that he had been won over by Carlow—the side of himself that Carlow was able to display to high-minded old-fashioned persons when he met them far away from a racecourse or a gaming table. She had always blamed the Chalkeys for pressing her to marry him; it now struck her that the country parson and his wife might have been genuinely taken in.

As she walked home with Hugh, she could not resist asking him, "What do you suppose has really happened to Mr. Chivers?"

"Some sort of accident, I expect. It is hard to imagine exactly what. If he isn't heard of in the next hour or so, we shall have to organize a search party."

But of course they would not find him, thought Rosalba, for she was convinced that Carlow must be miles away by now. She was a little surprised at his going off so abruptly, but Meade had insisted that his arrival would give the black sheep of the Carlow family a most unpleasant shock; it now turned out that he had been successfully beguiling an innocent young woman into a false marriage, in order to get his hands on her money. Rosalba had an idea that the attempt itself might be a criminal offense. If so, she could understand why he had taken to his heels.

The rest of the day was taken up with conversations about the missing man and efforts to find him. Hugh and William and several others went out on horseback to look for him with no result.

While the riders were gone, Mr. Sturdy called on the general and was closeted with him for some time.

"He has been examining Chivers's papers," the general told the rest of the family that evening. "Mrs. Copley wished that someone would take charge of them, and Sturdy, being a justice of the peace, considered himself the proper person.

151

I think he wanted me to approve of his action, in case Chivers objects when he does return."

Here General Rainham broke off to trim a guttering candle, and Rosalba felt her nerves tightening with apprehension once again. She had not thought of this.

"Did he discover anything useful, sir?" asked Hugh.

"Nothing. Apparently there were some documents relating to the West Indian property, but no letters from friends or relatives in England, which is what Sturdy was looking for."

Rosalba breathed a secret sigh of relief. She should have guessed that Carlow's disappearance had been carefully planned, though it did seem rather odd that he had left most of his clothes behind; Mr. Sturdy had inspected them in Mrs. Copley's best bedchamber.

The Rainhams agreed that the whole thing was a mystery.

"I never met the young man," said Alicia in her hesitant way, "but I suppose it is possible that he was a little unsteady. I hope not, for Miss Dorothy's sake, but it seems to me that he might have given way to some wild impulse, without ever considering the anxiety he would cause. Such things do happen."

"I never met the young man either," replied Hugh, "but I cannot believe that he had much chance of getting into bad company in Trilbourne yesterday between four and seven o'clock. There were no convivial drinking parties at either of the inns, only one stranger staying at the Sun, and he seems to have been a quiet person who received no visitors and left this morning in a post chaise. Dan Robinson dined at home— I asked his brother—and I can't think of any other local runagates who might have been acceptable companions to a man like Chivers."

So Meade had left the town, for he must have been the quiet person in the post chaise. Hearing this satisfied Rosalba that he had got rid of Carlow. Her relief was overshadowed by the question: what was she to do now?

Since the moment she had known for certain that Carlow was still alive (was it only yesterday?) she had been putting off the necessity of telling Hugh. Because she was afraid to let him discover what a sordid situation she had dragged him into, afraid of his sharp tongue, a possible outburst of impatience and disgust against the whole wretched business. All the same, she had taken it for granted that he would have to be told, if only because she was expecting Carlow to come and ask for money. She had not really believed that John Meade would be able to get rid of him.

However, she had misjudged Meade, and now that Carlow had gone away, couldn't she just remain silent, let Hugh go on believing that her first husband was dead and that their marriage was valid?

But she knew that she ought to tell him, especially as she now suspected that he might regret the impulsive chivalry which had induced him to marry her. Or was that suspicion simply a phantom she had created out of a too sensitive imagination? He had seemed easy and happy with her this morning; perhaps they would recover their old footing when he could shed some of his responsibilities and had more time to spare. But what would happen if it came out that she was still bound in law to her first husband?

His relations in Trilbourne had all been so kind to her; they had accepted her as Hugh's wife, and those things in her earlier life which they could not condone they had somehow managed to ignore or even forget. Once they learned that she was *not* Hugh's wife, they would no longer be able to accept her. They might be genuinely sorry, but they would have to act according to their religious and moral scruples. And Hugh himself? She was pretty certain that he would refuse to deceive his relations by pretending that the marriage was valid once he knew it wasn't. He would think that was dishonorable, and of course he would be right.

If the truth came out, she would probably have to return to Hunsden Street—which was what she had been wanting to do a week ago, only everything would be different, for she would be alone in London, separated from Hugh, who could not be with her even if he wished, for he had committed himself to remaining in Derbyshire so that he could battle with retrenchments and economies on the encumbered estate, while helping and advising Alicia.

And once Hugh was settled in Trilbourne, Rosalba decided, she would have lost him. It was a terrible temptation she had to face, all the worse because it was so easy. She simply had to keep quiet and do nothing.

She managed to keep to this sensible plan, though with some painful pricking of her conscience next morning, which was Sunday, while she sat facing Hugh in the square family pew which occupied the place of honor in the parish church. The box pew had seats all round it and a space in the middle; the ladies faced east, and the men sat with their backs to the horses, as William put it irreverently.

"We have left undone those things which we ought to have done," recited the congregation, and Rosalba felt plunged in guilt.

After the service they all assembled in the churchyard, where neat rows of tombstones ran between the phalanxes of yew trees, massively rounded and almost black; there were nearly a hundred of them, but it was said that no one who counted them could ever reach the same number twice. The gentry families greeted each other outside the west door. There was still no news and poor Dorothy Lumm looked pale and exhausted, but she had an idea, and a request.

"I have been thinking of places where Ned might have gone, and I began to wonder whether perhaps he decided to explore the woods around Ashwin. He loves a fine prospect and is so much interested in that noble old house—we had planned to make an expedition there someday, do you remember, Lettice? Suppose he went there alone and hurt himself in some way? There would be no one to hear him if he called for help. Could the place be searched?"

"It's true a man might easily take a toss over there," admitted the general. "What with fallen trees and hidden ditches and everything shockingly overgrown."

George Robinson, the agent, said in an undertone to Hugh, "I'm afraid there are some mantraps as well. Sir Augustus said they were the cheapest protection against intruders—that was after he told me to dismiss the caretaker."

It was agreed that a search party should set out for Ashwin, even though it was a Sunday, for such an errand of mercy could not be described as sabbath-breaking; there were good precedents in the New Testament.

There were plenty of volunteers.

"And I will come with you," exclaimed Dorothy. "You will drive me there, won't you, dear Mr. Sturdy?"

The magistrate looked horrified, and several of the other men joined with him in trying to discourage her from going to Ashwin; they were all thinking of what they might find there. But she refused to be put off, and Mrs. Lumm, who should have had some authority, seemed unable to exert it.

After some argument, Hugh said to Rosalba, "Will you come as well? To keep Miss Dorothy company."

"Yes, of course."

She felt very uncomfortable about the whole expedition, even though she was the one person who did not expect to find some horrid or distressing sight awaiting them. She had only just begun to realize how much extra strain her silence was imposing on the wretched Dorothy. It's wicked, she thought, to let her go on imagining that some terrible and mysterious fate has overtaken the man she loves. Yet would Dorothy be any less unhappy if she was told the truth?

Men and boys of every sort drove or rode or walked to Ashwin to join the search. Some had already patrolled the riverbanks for several miles. Although a man might fall into the Tirrel without leaving traces, his body would come to the surface sooner or later. Equally, the rough hillside above and below Ashwin was worth combing thoroughly, for it had become a wilderness where anything might lie undiscovered for days.

The carriage stopped outside the gatehouse, as before, but they were not going through into the courtyard today. Rosalba saw Dorothy and Mr. Sturdy pacing the terrace below the high stone wall and went to join them.

"Ah, here is Mrs. Hugh Rainham come to take care of you," said Mr. Sturdy. "You will not think me uncivil if I leave you together? I want to see what the men are doing up in the woods."

He hobbled away, leaning heavily on his stick. Rosalba thought he looked old and tired.

"He is afraid I am going to have the vapors," remarked Dorothy.

"I am sure you are far too sensible," said Rosalba bracingly, though she was not at all sure.

Dorothy was restless and nervous. She said, "I wanted to help them look for Ned, but it seems that females are not required."

"We might find the ground rather too steep, besides being very uneven," said Rosalba tactfully.

She herself was wearing stout boots and had changed into an old skirt and petticoat that could be bunched up in one hand for country walking, but she noticed that Dorothy was still in the frilled chintz and thin slippers she had worn at church. One step off the terrace and she'd tear her dress or twist her ankle.

"I suppose you are right."

Dorothy started down the hillside. Between the terrace and the river there had once been one of those stiff, ornamental parterres that were now so old-fashioned, as well as an orchard and a vegetable garden. Now the briers and bracken that grew outside the domain had come in to obliterate the pattern of ordered cultivation, strangling plants and shrubs, hiding dangerous dips and steps, smothering everything that had been delicate and rare with a commonplace, unlovely fertility. Several men were beating their way through this derelict garden, while others could be seen working their way through the deep bracken that ran over the rest of the hillside. Rosalba could also see George Robinson moving on a circular course of his own, a little beyond the other searchers; she thought he was probably inspecting the mantraps. She also caught sight of his brother, Dan, wielding a rake. She wondered whether he really expected to find his friend Carlow—or whether, like her, he knew this whole performance was a farce.

There was a crumbling stone bench at the end of the terrace, padded with a springy cushion of young green ivy. Rosalba suggested to Dorothy that they might sit down. The sun had gone in, but the day was hot and airless; the clouds seemed to be sitting only a few feet above the top of the hill.

"I think we are going to have a storm."

"If Ned is lying out in the open, he will be drenched to the skin."

Rosalba felt like a criminal.

She said, "Do you think it is possible that we have all

156

jumped to the wrong conclusion? That Mr. Chivers was called away suddenly, perhaps on some urgent matter of business? He might have written a note for you that has gone astray."

"He wouldn't have gone without taking any of his clothes," objected Dorothy, not unreasonably.

She began to talk about her dearest Ned.

Rosalba listened at first with feelings of guilt and compassion, which presently changed to extreme irritation. What a goose the girl must be, to believe such a lot of moonshine about Carlow! Of course he must have worked hard at his part as the devoted lover of such a considerable heiress; she had some excuse for her raptures about his fine appearance, charming manners and sweetness of temper—no one's temper could seem sweeter than Carlow's if it served his purpose—but all this stuff about his noble sentiments, his serious views on religion, this must be the greatest humbug. Carlow was an irreligious cynic, and though he might pose as a man of principle, Rosalba did not think he had said half the fine things he was credited with. This silly girl had molded him to suit her own fancy.

Perhaps Dorothy sensed that she had a rather skeptical listener, for after a while she got up and walked away along the terrace. A few minutes later Rosalba too stood up. I shall have to tell them, she thought. Abstractedly she began to walk in the other direction. She came to a mossy flight of steps, climbed precariously down them into a corner of the old knot garden overrun with nettles. She came to a halt, losing all connection with time as she tried to sort out her difficulties.

Until she heard Hugh's voice behind her saying sharply, "Rosalba!"

He was at the top of the steps, weary and disheveled and plainly in a bad temper.

"What the devil are you doing down there? Why did you leave Dorothy Lumm?"

"I thought she wanted to be alone."

"Very likely. But the whole point of your coming here was that there should be another woman with her if she had to withstand a painful shock."

Rosalba swallowed. She almost said that Dorothy was not

going to be overcome by any distressing discoveries at Ashwin. But this was not the moment to make her confession. Hugh had come down to her level, and she saw that his hands were scratched and blistered, no doubt from forcing a path through the briers. None of the men who had spent the last two hours in extreme discomfort would want to hear at this moment that they had been wasting their time.

"I'll go to Dorothy," she said.

"There's no need. We've found no sign of Chivers's having been here, and Sturdy has driven her home. But I still think you might have taken more care of the poor girl, shown some sympathy for what she must be suffering. I don't know what's come over you these days. You seem entirely wrapped up in your own concerns."

This was too much.

"How do you know what I am thinking about?" she retorted angrily. "You hardly notice my existence!"

"I've noticed one thing," he said grimly. "Since I brought you to Derbyshire as my wife—since the moment I put the ring on your finger in fact—you have hardly taken the smallest trouble to consider my wishes or to please me in any way."

"That's a lie!" she almost screamed at him. "I've tried my hardest—what is there for me to do when you neglect me and ignore me and spend all your time talking about rents and mortgages—"

"Good God, must you be so childish?" He was getting colder and more infuriatingly reasonable as she grew hotter. "You know I feel obliged to set the estate to rights for Alicia and Theo. If I hadn't quarreled with Gus, I might have been able to exercise some control—"

"Oh, what nonsense! You couldn't have stopped his gaming and drinking, no one could. But I suppose I am to blame for your quarrel, because you knocked him down for blackening my character. Perhaps you regret that now. Perhaps you even wonder whether some of his stories were true."

"Surely not," he drawled in a voice of icy contempt. "No woman with your passion for respectability sells herself merely for money."

She could not fathom the undercurrents of this last remark, but she knew that he was trying to hurt her. They stared at each other with the bitter hostility only possible between those who have been in love. Then she turned and walked away from him, pushing through the jungle of the old deserted garden, hardly aware of the thorns and the choked nettles, the ruts that jarred her feet, or the white roses—her own name flowers—poised like butterflies on the sprawling, overgrown bushes as she passed.

She did not stop until she came to the river. Then she paused, the tears running down her cheeks. Where to go? She could hear men's voices on the hill above her; the search party was breaking up. She was not going back there to be quizzed by everyone; they'd all see she had been crying, and she did not want to be driven home by Hugh either. She could walk along the riverbank to Bridge Place; it was not very far, following a much more direct line than the carriage road, which took a wide loop.

She started walking again, doggedly, without looking to right or left, indifferent to the heat and the flies, the beauties of the smooth, grassy valley, the sparkling water and the tall, graceful trees. Trees and grass had that very vivid green intensity in contrast to the sky which had now become as heavy as pewter. There was going to be a storm. She could hardly fail to realize that, but she did not care. She could not allow herself to feel or think, just to put one foot in front of the other and go on until it was time to stop.

She had reached the new bridge when the first rain fell in solitary splashing drops. It would have been wise to shelter under the arches; however, she pressed on. She hurried along the stretch of river she had come to know very well, below the gardens of the town houses and past the lane where she had seen Carlow on that memorable afternoon ten days ago. By now it was raining fairly hard, and in spite of her misery, the rain acted on her in the traditional fashion of cold water, restoring her common sense: she would not improve matters by getting soaked. She was drawing near the deserted ferryman's cottage. Standing under the eaves for shelter, she saw that the door was broken so that it did not shut properly: the best way to keep dry would be to go inside.

She pushed the old, warped door and went in. It was not a very agreeable haven, just an earth floor and four peeling walls. There was no furniture, naturally enough, though a row of sacks against the far wall suggested that someone had been sleeping here. Now she looked again, the sacks appeared to be spread like a blanket rather than a mattress, for they were humped as though someone was lying asleep underneath them; some drunken vagabond perhaps? There was a curiously unpleasant smell in the cottage, though she could hear no sound of breathing. She stood still, straining doubtfully at the shadowy outline of the sacks. Then she saw a faint glitter in the darkest corner. It was a shoe buckle. And now she could discern the actual shape of the shoe, made of polished black leather, not the kind of shoe to be worn by a vagrant.

Stepping forward, she pulled away the nearest sack and found herself looking straight down into those blue eyes which had often seemed to her so empty—but never so empty as now, glaring china-blue out of a face that was fallen away and waxen, apart from the rosette of purple and red swelling across the left temple, and the trickle of dried blood at the left ear and nostril.

For an instant Rosalba was petrified with shock. Then panic seized her and she rushed out of the cottage into the rain. She hardly knew what she was doing, almost felt that the body could not be real; it was a sinister hallucination to punish her for letting everyone search for a man who wasn't dead.

Only he *was* dead. That dreadful sight was no trick of the nerves.

Someone had stopped her, a man carrying an open umbrella.

"Mrs. Rainham, what has happened? What is the matter?"

She discovered she was clinging to the arm of Mr. Sturdy, talking nonsense.

As soon as he made out what she was trying to say, he gave her the umbrella and went to the cottage himself. A moment later he returned.

"It's Ned Chivers. He's dead."

"Yes, but how did he...how was he...killed?"

"I don't know," said Mr. Sturdy. "I shall have to find out."

10

Rosalba sat in Mr. Sturdy's bookroom, her teeth chattering against the rim of the brandy glass she was holding in her shaking hand. She was shivering purely from shock, for though she felt cold, this must be a delusion: in spite of the heat of the day Mr. Sturdy had insisted on having a fire lit for her, to offset the dangers of a wet skirt and damp shoes. The room was like a bakehouse.

He had escorted her indoors through the little gate at the end of his garden and up the sloping lawn. He had tried to soothe her in a worried, fatherly voice, saying how lucky it was that he had come out in the rain to make sure that some of his rare plants were not getting waterlogged in their china tubs. (It was not clear whether he had meant to stand over them with his open umbrella.) He had sent for Mr. Roberts, the apothecary, who had taken Rosalba's pulse and prescribed hartshorn before hurrying on to the ferryman's cottage. Rosalba had rejected the hartshorn in favor of brandy.

"And I have let them know at Bridge Place," added Mr. Sturdy, regarding her gravely. "I daresay Hugh will be here directly."

"How very kind of you, sir," murmured Rosalba, wishing he had not done this but unable to say so.

But when Hugh arrived he was very different from the bitter stranger she had parted from at Ashwin. He hurried into the room, looking distracted. His eyes flew to Rosalba, and he took her hand, saying, "My dear girl, what a horrid experience you have had. I am so sorry."

"It was very disagreeable," she said, not daring to meet his eye. "But I am better now, and Mr. Sturdy has been so kind."

"I am most grateful to you, sir," said Hugh. "But I couldn't quite make out your message. Rosalba found Chivers dead in the ferryman's cottage, but how did he come to be there? How did he die?"

Mr. Sturdy pursed up his mouth and said nothing, as

161

though to indicate that Hugh should have more consideration for his wife's nerves.

Hugh took the hint, asking her: "Is this too distressing? Would you rather not talk about it?"

He had seated himself beside her and was gently holding her hand.

"I don't mind," she said.

In fact, she wanted to hear what conclusion the men would come to.

"He had received a severe blow on the side of the head," said the magistrate noncommittally.

"And then went into the cottage and died there? How very odd. Or was the body placed there after death? I think I'll go and take a look," said Hugh, beginning to get up.

"Please don't leave me," whispered Rosalba in sudden alarm.

"Not if you don't wish it, my love."

He immediately gave up the plan and remained where he was, pandering to what must have seemed like ridiculous feminine fears without any sign of irritation. The tenderness in his voice made her feel horribly guilty, but she dared not let him find out the truth at this moment. Her ideas were in a turmoil. She had to think. The men went on talking. Mr. Sturdy was only waiting for the apothecary's report before going to break the news to the Lumms, a task he dreaded. He limped about his crowded room, leaning on his ebony cane. There were books and papers everywhere, overflowing the shelves and covering every table and most of the chairs. The walls were hung with theatrical prints, mostly illustrating his passion for Shakespeare. Presently a servant came in to say that Mr. Roberts had returned from the ferryman's cottage.

The men went to talk to him in the adjoining room, Hugh saying to Rosalba, "You won't mind, will you? I shall be quite close."

She managed to imply that she was perfectly calm now, not afraid of being left alone. As soon as they had closed the door, she tiptoed across and carefully opened it a crack, so that she could hear what was being said.

"...such a blow would have been instantly fatal." It was

the apothecary speaking. "Or at least would have rendered him instantly unconscious, incapable of further action or movement. . . . And I do not see how such a thing could have happened accidentally. As far as I can judge he was hit with some kind of cudgel. There was no suitable weapon in the cottage."

"He must have been attacked and robbed," began Mr. Sturdy.

"I beg your pardon, sir: he was not robbed. He had a purse on him with several guineas in it, as well as his watch and fob. I have them here. Will you take charge of them?"

"I suppose I had better do so. Were there any papers?"

"None, sir."

Hugh asked, "How long do you reckon he's been dead?"

"The best part of two days, Mr. Rainham. Judging from the condition of the corpse."

"That takes us back to the evening of his disappearance—which is what one might expect."

Rosalba moved silently back to her chair. She had heard what she needed to know, and her heart sank. For by now she had disentangled the suspicion which had made her go on instinctively guarding the secret of Carlow's identity. She thought she could guess who had killed him.

John Meade had promised to get rid of him for her, and that was what he had done.

It was an awful possibility, but what else was she to think? He knew he was to blame for the dilemma he had placed her in, and she had done nothing to lessen his remorse. He loved her, he wanted to protect her, and she now thought he had been overconfident when he said he could frighten Carlow away. Suppose in the course of their meeting, Carlow had somehow discovered Meade's Achilles heel—his fondness for Rosalba—and threatened to ruin her. Meade might very likely have struck out violently, in a burst of anger. Or even if he acted in cold blood, she thought, he did it for me, and I cannot be the one to give him away.

Hugh and Mr. Sturdy came back into the bookroom and gave her a watered-down version of what the apothecary had said.

"Of course we know very little about Edward Chivers,"

163

remarked Hugh. "He may have had enemies who followed him here. He may even have had enemies in Trilbourne."

"Dan Robinson!" exclaimed Mr. Sturdy. "I'll wager he's at the bottom of this."

Hugh and Rosalba were surprised. In her case there was an unpleasant sense of foreboding.

"Dan Robinson!" repeated Hugh. "What had he to do with Chivers? I did not realize they were particularly acquainted."

"Well, they were better acquainted than you think. Thick as thieves. That's the most apt description, and when thieves fall out, you know—"

"But I thought you considered Chivers a young man of exemplary character; that is what I understood you to say, sir."

"So I did at first. As it turns out, I was grossly deceived. I can't explain in detail—not without betraying a confidence." Mr. Sturdy had gone very red in the face. He looked portentous. "People confide in me, you know. In my position."

Rosalba wondered rather desperately who in Trilbourne had discovered a connection between Dan Robinson and the so-called Chivers—the kind of connection they wished to discuss with a magistrate. Hugh was still looking very puzzled. He said he must take his wife home.

Mr. Sturdy offered them the use of his carriage, but the rain had stopped, and Rosalba said quickly that she would be glad of a breath of air. The bookroom was by now quite stifling.

The bells of the parish church had just finished pealing for evensong when they stepped into the High Street, and there was hardly a soul about.

Hugh gave Rosalba his arm and said, "We are friends again, are we not? I am afraid I was very cross this afternoon, but I did not mean one half of what I said, and I don't suppose you did either."

If he could describe his lethal attack on her as being very cross she thought he must have an extremely short memory, but she was touched by his tender concern for her, he was so much more like the Hugh she had known in London, and she was as sensitive to kindness from him as she was to his anger or indifference.

So she said, "You were right to blame me for not taking proper care of Dorothy Lumm."

"You never expected us to find Chivers at Ashwin, did you? Dead or alive."

She was startled. "What makes you think so?"

"You had a skeptical look in your eye, as though you thought the poor fellow's passion for fine prospects might have been exaggerated. Dorothy considers Ashwin highly romantic, and he probably agreed with her without wishing to walk out there and wander about the place on his own."

I ought to tell him now, she thought. If only I could be sure he would keep quiet about John Meade. One could never tell what scruples a man would have where the law was concerned. Of course, Rosalba herself would not wish to sit back and say nothing while some other person was accused by Mr. Sturdy in a fit of magisterial zeal, but she thought this was fairly unlikely. She was becoming more and more convinced that the unfortunate Meade had been driven to extreme lengths by remorse and desperation. And it was no good; she could not help feeling a great deal sorrier for him than she did for Carlow. Surely they could let sleeping dogs lie?

"Hugh," she began, doubtful and tentative.

Her voice was so soft that apparently he did not hear her. She looked up at him and saw that she had lost his attention. His eyes were remote, as though he was intent on something a long way off. With a flicker of relief she decided that this was not the right moment.

At Bridge Place she was cosseted and made much of. Everyone was horrified by the violent crime that had been committed so close at hand, and the idea of Rosalba's stumbling on the body was shocking to them all. Lettice was in floods of tears over the death of the handsome young man who was engaged to her friend.

"How dreadful it is for Dorothy! I cannot bear to think of what she is suffering now."

I keep forgetting Dorothy, thought Rosalba with compunction. I ought to be more sorry for her. I *am* sorry for her—but what a lucky escape she has had!

She went to bed early and slept much better than she expected, from sheer exhaustion.

When the maid brought her chocolate in the morning, there was a note on the tray, folded up very small. Rosalba smoothed it out and read the bald message.

> *I must speak with you on a matter of the greatest urgency. Will wait under the great tree on the far side of the bridge.*   *D.R.*

She might have guessed that she would hear from Dan Robinson before long. She took the lid off the tall, fluted cup and tried to drink her chocolate, though it was still scalding hot. When she had swallowed about two-thirds of the dark, cloying liquid, she left it and got up to dress, without waiting for the ministrations of her maid.

On the landing she was intercepted by Alicia, who wanted a comfortable conference about Theo. Once that was over she managed to slip out of the house like a conspirator—after all, she was a conspirator. Five minutes later she was crossing the ancient stone bridge.

She knew very well where to go. On the far side of the river there was a gigantic horse chestnut with branches curving down to the ground, concealing anyone who stood underneath. As she parted clusters of leaves, she saw Dan Robinson leaning against the massive trunk of the tree.

"Well," she said, "I've come. What do you want?"

"Your help. I have to leave Trilbourne and I need money."

"Oh, I thought we should come to the question of money pretty soon. If you are asking me to buy your silence—"

"It's not that," he interrupted her. He sounded husky and uneasy, not his usual smooth self. "I am in danger of being arrested for the murder of your husband."

"Good heavens, why?"

"That old fool Sturdy has got his knife into me. I've told him I was at home all Friday, but he won't listen."

"And did you kill Carlow?"

This was disingenuous, for of course he would insist he was innocent. He did, though in a rather disconcerting way.

"Oddly enough I was about to ask you the same question."

It took Rosalba a few seconds to grasp this. The suggestion was so utterly unexpected.

"You cannot suppose I had anything to do with his death!"

"You had a stronger motive than anyone else. I had no reason at all. I was his friend—the only one he had, poor devil. But you must have wanted him dead. In the circumstances."

She could hardly deny this. She said, "I couldn't have struck such a blow."

"A woman can use force if she has to. And he would have allowed you to come close enough."

Rosalba began to feel sick.

"If you go on threatening me—"

"Do try to understand. I'm not saying you killed him. I'm simply saying that you had a better reason than anyone else, except perhaps your—your paramour, which is what I'm afraid we must call Mr. Hugh Rainham. But I have a notion that he has been kept in the dark all along. Am I right?"

She nodded, thankful now that she had kept her secret.

"The venerable Sturdy is also in the dark on that subject. He seems to think that the late Mr. Chivers and I had some illicit dealings together—heaven knows what can have given him that idea!—and that I made away with him after a quarrel we had over the division of the spoils."

And perhaps that was exactly what had happened. All the same, Rosalba did not believe it. Bad as they both were, Carlow and Dan had always been allied. And while Carlow was trying to marry Miss Lumm, she did not see him risking a quarrel with a man who knew he was married already.

"If I am arrested," Dan continued, "I shall have to defend myself as best I can by pointing out that there is another person in Trilbourne with a far better reason for the murder than I. You can hardly blame me for that. I daresay a true gentleman would keep silent and hang, but I am not cast in that heroic mold."

Peering at him through the green gloom, she saw that in spite of his jaunty manner he was sweating with fear.

"What do you want me to do?"

"Give me some money so that I can disappear. I'm in low water, as it happens, and there's no one else I can turn to.

My brother won't help. I'm afraid my family gets progressively less generous as life goes on."

Rosalba could believe that. She said, "I haven't got any money."

"You could get hold of some."

She tried to think. It seemed to her that she had either to help Dan get away or come out with the whole story. That would involve John Meade. She could not steel herself to such a betrayal. Whatever he had done, he had done out of love for her. How could she inform against him?

"Tell me," she asked, "why did you bring Carlow here? Was it so that he could make Miss Lumm fall in love with him?"

He seemed genuinely astonished. "Lord, no—that was quite unexpected."

So what had that precious pair really been up to, and who was it that had confided in Mr. Sturdy that the estimable Mr. Chivers was a wolf in sheep's clothing? At this moment it hardly mattered. The important thing was that Dan should leave Trilbourne as soon as he had the means.

"You wait here," said Rosalba, "and I'll see what I can do."

As she sped back across the sunlit bridge, she was already working out a plan.

When they first arrived in Derbyshire General Rainham had given Hugh the sole use of the small study leading off the library and containing a bureau-bookcase in which he could keep all the papers relating to the Ashwin estate, of which he was now the trustee. In the bureau there was a secret cache for money and jewelry, a convenience often provided by cabinetmakers to outwit light-fingered servants as well as professional thieves. Rosalba had seen Hugh stowing away a reserve fund there, for use in an emergency. She was going to help herself to some of that money and give it to Dan Robinson. She did not think that Hugh would notice at once that it was missing, and in a day or two, once Dan was safely out of the way, she would tell him the truth, all except the part that concerned Meade. She would pretend she had paid Robinson merely because she was afraid of the scandal, and if Hugh thought this very craven of her, there would be nothing he could do about it.

Bridge Place was bathed in a morning calm which suggested that most of the family had gone out. She made her way to the study, let down the flap of the bureau and touched the concealed spring. A section of tiny drawers swung forward on a hinge, revealing behind them a small cavity which contained a single sheet of folded paper and a leather bag full of gold coins.

Rosalba was wearing the usual linen pocket under her dress; it hung on a long tape from her waist and could be reached through a slit in her skirt. She pulled it out and filled it from the bag of gold. The pocket was now very heavy, and she was afraid it might make a clinking noise as she walked. Perhaps she could pad the coins with something soft. She picked up the piece of paper that had been lying in the cache and looked to see if it was of any value. She saw it was a letter addressed to Hugh and was about to replace it when her eye fell on the signature and she had yet another shock.

Henry Carlow. It was a name she knew very well, though she had never met the owner—her husband's eldest brother. She began to read with a sinking dismay. It was written from the family home in Devonshire and dated several days after her wedding at St. George's, Hanover Square.

Hugh Rainham Esq.

My dear Sir,

I have today read in the newspaper the announcement of your marriage to the widow of the late Edgar Carlow. As far as I am aware, my brother is alive and at present residing in New England. He was married some two years ago to a Miss Rosalba York, an orphan, then living in the care of relations in Suffolk. I never had the pleasure of meeting this lady, but if she has received news of my brother's death, I should be most grateful if you would inform me of the details, as no report of this event has yet been conveyed to me nor, I can confidently state, to my attorney, Mr. John Meade of Lincoln's Inn.

I am, my dear sir, your most obliged servant,

Henry Carlow.

Rosalba sat for some time staring at the written lines though no longer seeing them. A faint sound behind her made her turn her head. Hugh was standing in the doorway, watching her. He had taken in the open bureau, the secret hiding place, the letter in her hand. There was no longer any sense in pretending.

"So you knew," she said. "You've known all along."

"Since the day after we arrived here. That letter followed me from town." He spoke in a hard, practical voice which was charged suddenly with a note of anguish. "Why did you do it, Rosalba? Why did you lie about his death? Didn't you believe you could trust me unless I believed I was married to you?"

11

"It wasn't a lie," she said. "I honestly believed he'd been drowned. And I must say, Hugh, considering what mistakes can be made over news coming from a great distance, I think you might have given me the benefit of the doubt. Why didn't you show me Henry Carlow's letter?"

"Because it wasn't a question of a false report, some confusion over the name of a man lost at sea. There can have been no such report. You told me you had it from Meade, yet the Carlow family, his own clients, had heard nothing."

Now she saw what a tangle Meade's well-meaning deception had got her into.

She said, "It's true John Meade never told Carlow's brother he'd been drowned. But he did tell me. He made it all up and convinced me I was a widow, because he hoped I might agree to marry him."

Hugh stared at her.

"What a damned stupid thing to do—let alone the impudence of it. Had you given him any encouragement?"

"Of course not. But he was distressed by what he thought of as my irregular situation, and it never crossed his mind that you might make an honest woman of me. I daresay he foresaw the difficulties better than we did."

There was a longish silence after this.

Then Hugh said, "I'm sorry. I see I have treated you very shabbily. Will you forgive me?"

The real explanation of all his recent moods and cryptic remarks had just dawned on her. She felt cheapened and resentful.

"If you thought I had tricked you into a false marriage for the advantage of using your name and spending your money—"

"I never thought that, Rosalba. I thought you did it for Anne. To safeguard her so that she could never be ousted by my marrying anyone else and having legitimate children. I know you've always been afraid that one day I should leave you."

This infuriated her, partly because it was true.

"You flatter yourself," she said. "I wish now I had married John Meade."

"Unfortunately you are not in a position to marry anyone."

She realized that he still did not know the whole truth.

"When did you find out that Meade was lying to you?" he asked.

Without reflecting, she said, "He told me so last week."

The admission had slipped out; it was too late to recall it. Naturally he pounced on what she had said.

"What was Meade doing in Trilbourne? Has he fresh news of Carlow? Do you know where he is now?"

She told him.

This had the effect of really disturbing his intolerable poise. He looked almost stunned.

"Oh, my God!" he said in a low voice.

He asked a few more questions and soon had the whole story. He sat down in a tall wing chair and remained unnaturally still, his expression closed and guarded. She did not know what he was thinking.

Presently he said, "There's only one thing we can do. We must go and see Sturdy and you'll have to tell him everything."

"No, Hugh!" she exclaimed. "I can't do that!"

171

"If you don't, Dan Robinson will."

"Not if we give him the money to go away."

"It's too late. The constable was out looking for him an hour ago. There'll be a general hue and cry."

Rosalba wanted to run across the bridge with her bag of gold, but realized that Hugh was probably right.

"What am I to do?" she asked unhappily. "I won't incriminate John Meade."

She half expected Hugh to say that this was quixotic nonsense. He was unlikely to feel much sympathy for Meade on any grounds.

To her surprise, however, he said, "There is no need for you to mention him, nor your glimpse of Carlow walking along the riverbank. You had better say you had no idea of his having been alive or in Trilbourne until you recognized his body in the ferryman's cottage. That will remove any ambiguity."

Rosalba felt dimly that there was a flaw here, though she was not sure what it was. She consented very unwillingly to go and see Mr. Sturdy, since Hugh was so determined that this was what she ought to do and she was used to accepting his advice.

Mr. Sturdy's untidy bookroom was mercifully not so hot as it had been yesterday. He himself, looking worn and distracted, was at first too busy giving orders to attend to them. He took his duties as a justice of the peace very seriously and had evidently decided that no one else in Trilbourne had the authority or the ability to deal with a case of murder. It was only when Hugh announced that they had some vital information that he gave them his full attention. Rosalba wished Hugh would not be so insistent. She felt strangely unreal, detached from her surroundings, as though she was acting in a play she did not greatly care for. Perhaps this idea was suggested by Mr. Sturdy's passionate interest in the theater. On the wall opposite there was a print depicting Lady Macbeth in the sleepwalking scene.

Mr. Sturdy faced them across his overladen table.

"My wife wishes to make a statement," said Hugh.

She noticed that he still called her his wife.

"A statement, madam?"

172

"I should have told you yesterday, sir," faltered Rosalba, "that I recognized the—the victim of the murderous attack. The person you called Edward Chivers. His real name was Edgar Carlow. He was my first—that is to say, he was my husband."

"Your husband? But this is incredible—I cannot believe it!"

Mr. Sturdy seemed truly appalled. In fact, he spent the next five minutes trying to persuade Rosalba that she must be mistaken. No doubt the dead man bore some slight resemblance to her late husband which had been exaggerated by shock. She had seen him for only a brief moment in a bad light.

As Rosalba had concealed her earlier sight of Carlow, she did not know what to say. She glanced at Hugh.

He said: "There is someone else in Trilbourne who knows the dead man's true name. Daniel Robinson."

"That villain! I shall soon have him under lock and key."

"He has already pointed out to my—to Rosalba that she had a better motive than anyone for getting rid of Carlow. Whereas he himself has absolutely none. And I don't think you can prove otherwise."

Surely there was no need for Hugh to have said that? Rosalba had begun to shake again, in that curious disjointed way she had been shaking yesterday after she found the body. She could not keep her hands still in her lap. Mr. Sturdy rose and began to limp up and down his room. He had not bothered to arm himself with his usual support, the long ebony cane topped by the silver hand holding a ball of polished marble. It was leaning against his chair.

"Such a suggestion is quite outrageous!" he boomed at his most magisterial. "No woman could have struck such a blow."

"Is that what Roberts says?"

"Yes. No. Well, not precisely. In any case, there is another candidate. If I understand this extraordinary affair correctly, if the dead man was legally married to Mrs. Rainham—Mrs. Carlow—then you yourself had an excellent reason for wanting to be rid of him."

Rosalba held her breath.

Hugh had gone very white. Leaning back, he pushed his

173

chair a few inches further from hers and turned slightly away from her, seeming to leave her unprotected.

At last he said, "I spent the whole of Friday afternoon and evening in the company of my uncle and my cousin William."

This was a nightmare. She had never suspected Hugh of killing Carlow, but surely any man would want to shield the woman he loved—or had loved? Instead of behaving as though he wanted her to be accused of murder.

Mr. Sturdy thought so too.

"You are strangely lacking in chivalry," he said severely, and when Hugh did not answer, he added, "No jury would convict her."

"I hope not, sir. But there are three months to go before the next Assizes. Derby Gaol in summer is notoriously unhealthy."

Rosalba closed her eyes. There was a constriction in her throat and a pressure against her ears, so that she hardly grasped the sense of Mr. Sturdy's words, spoken somewhere above her head with a kind of groan.

"What am I to do? How can I expose such a tender young creature to the perils of gaol fever, the society of thieves and harlots? I am in a grievous quandary."

"A quandary, sir?" There was a cold, implacable note in Hugh's voice which did pierce Rosalba's state of forlorn misery.

Mr. Sturdy threw himself down in his chair and covered his face with his hands.

"It was an accident, I swear it was an accident! I struck him in anger but I never meant to kill him!"

Rosalba was left gaping in astonishment. There was a curious sound from Hugh, something like a sigh of relief.

He said, "What angered you, sir? Was it his attempt to marry Dorothy Lumm for her money?"

Mr. Sturdy took a little time to answer.

"I would have done my best to prevent that marriage, had he lived. Of course, I didn't know he was married already. But I knew nothing against him until that very day when he taunted me, jeered at my scholarship, said he could make me look a fool in the eyes of all those whose opinions I valued.

That was why I struck him. Pride, or vanity rather—that has been the ruin of me."

There was another pause. Mr. Sturdy sat haunched in his chair. His face, sagging in its creases, looked sickly and old.

Hugh moved nearer to Rosalba, whispering some plea she did not catch, and tried to take her hand. She shook him off. He had been cruel and unfeeling when she needed him, and she was not prepared to accept such an overture directly the strange turn of events revealed her innocence.

Mr. Sturdy began to speak. Words poured out of him as though he hoped that confession would be good for his soul, and Rosalba listened in a state of suspended animation, because the story he had to tell was a small distraction from her own misery.

"I have been engaged for some time in a reprehensible piece of lawbreaking, though I meant no harm by it. I intended nothing but good. As you know, I tried in vain to rent Ashwin from your cousin Augustus; I was much concerned over the state of the building and the contents; in particular I was afraid the documents in the muniment room might suffer. I said this one day to George Robinson in the presence of his brother. Afterwards Dan came to me privately and suggested he should remove some of these documents and bring them to me for safe custody. He could get hold of his brother's keys and enter the house when he chose. Well, I am afraid I listened to the voice of the serpent. I took everything he brought me and rewarded him for his pains."

"I knew someone had been in the muniment room," said Hugh. "But my dear sir, I hope this very minor peccadillo was not the cause of your getting into much graver difficulties? I'm sure that all my family would have appreciated your concern. All except Gus, that is, and I really think his puerile spite and irresponsibility justified your unorthodox methods."

Mr. Sturdy managed a wavering smile. "I am grateful for your forbearance, though indeed I never supposed that you would condemn me very severely. It was not simply the pillaging of your family papers that led to my downfall. The things Robinson brought me at first were of no particular value to anyone save an antiquarian like myself—rent rolls, inventories, leases and the like. Then one day he came to me in a state of high glee, saying he had discovered some items in a chest he had not opened before which looked more promising. I remember the evening he came, for I had been drinking tea with Mrs. Lumm across the way and she confided to me that little Dolly seemed much pleased with young Chivers, whom I myself had introduced to her the week before. At that time I saw no connection between this and the documents I was receiving from Ashwin."

"How should you?"

"How indeed?" said Mr. Sturdy sadly. "I had first come across Chivers in the church, looking at the Rainham family monuments. He professed a great interest in history, and I was thoroughly taken in. Flattered by his deference, I suppose. He egged me on to talk of my love of Shakespeare ...Meanwhile I was receiving a rich harvest from Robinson, and of course I was too blind to notice the coincidence. The new discoveries related to the Mistress Mary Hall who married one of your ancestors; there was a letter which seemed to prove her relationship to William Shakespeare's son-in-law, Dr. Hall of Stratford-upon-Avon. What's more, Robinson told me that the chest had been lined with sheets of parchment written over in some kind of old-fashioned script no longer in use. He brought me a sample. The writing was certainly Tudor. I could not recognize the hand, but no examples of the hand I was hoping for are known to exist, bar a few signatures. Once I began to read, I was sure the style was authentic. What I had in my possession was a fragment of an old play. There were certain names and references—in short, I believed I was about to recover Shakespeare's lost masterpiece, *The Noble History of King Arthur*."

Briefly, there was a sense of wonder and excitement in the bookroom, a totally different excitement. Carlow's sordid death was forgotten as all their imaginations were captured by that marvelous possibility.

Then Mr. Sturdy went on with his bitter chronicle. "It never crossed my mind that I was being swindled. The stuff was so convincing both in form and content. And how could Dan Robinson have forged a Jacobean play?"

The idea of forgery was a flint to light a spark in Rosalba's memory. Carlow in their London lodging, practicing Gus

Rainham's signature. Herself warning him that he could be hanged for that particular accomplishment. Suddenly she understood his part in the business.

"I was naturally elated," continued Mr. Sturdy. "At the same time I began to be very uneasy. I had, or thought I had, access to a literary treasure of untold value, yet I could not publish abroad my discovery without saying how I had come by it, and this was clearly impossible. I was at a loss what to do when I heard that Augustus was dead. Everything was now changed. I felt I had only to wait a little and I should be granted full access to the muniment room—at liberty to reveal everything that was, or ever had been, preserved there. I did not wish to display an unseemly haste, however, so I said nothing of my hopes, knowing what a number of urgent problems had been created by your cousin's death. When Robinson brought me another sheet of manuscript, I paid him for it, but said I required no more papers from Ashwin. He seemed very much cast down, and a week later he was back with more. This time I repeated quite sharply that our arrangement was at an end and he could expect nothing further from me. That was last Tuesday. On Friday Chivers—the man I knew as Chivers—came here in the late afternoon. He walked up through the garden and tapped on this window to be let in."

They all glanced at the long Venetian window with its view of the narrow, sloping lawn.

"I was a little surprised by his informality," said Mr. Sturdy, "but I let him in. I thought perhaps he had come to consult me on some matter connected with his approaching marriage. Instead he began to speak of my dealings with Dan Robinson, making it very plain that he was a party to the whole business. I was utterly astounded. He threatened to denounce me as Robinson's accomplice in crime unless I handed over a large sum of money. This made very unpleasant hearing, but I was not going to be frightened by such a rogue. I told him that in spite of the irregularity of my conduct, I did not believe any living member of the Rainham family would wish to prosecute me, and I added that the scales had fallen from my eyes and I could see he was not a fit person to marry Miss Lumm. After which he began to

177

make threats of an entirely different kind: he informed me that I had been duped, that the documents I valued so highly had been written by himself and that if he made this known I should become a laughingstock.

"At first I would not believe him. I said I had recognized the true touch of genius in passages from a play *King Arthur* and whatever his skill as a forger, he could not emulate our greatest poet. Whereupon he began to quote some of these lines, pointing out that they were borrowed from Shakespeare's lesser-known plays, with names altered to suit his fudged-up fraud. There was a quotation from *Coriolanus*— how I had missed it I don't know, only he had substituted Baden for Corioli. He began to mock me, saying that every literate person in the kingdom would hold me in contempt: the great Shakespearean scholar trapped by his own incompetence. That was when I lost my temper. He was sitting where you are now; I had risen in my agitation and was reaching for my stick. In a moment of unconsidering rage I hit him as hard as I could with the weighted handle."

He held the stick up now, and they studied the curious silver hand clasping the marble globe, its milky density veined in green. There was now a darker line curving over the polished surface, a faint crack caused by the violent impact of human bone.

There was a silence while they all three contemplated this ghastly evidence. Rosalba shuddered.

"What did you do then?" prompted Hugh.

"I was horrified. Overcome by the dreadful thing I had done. Not that I felt any great pity for that scoundrel, but still, to take a human life—I who had always been the most peaceable of men. And I remembered too that this was Dorothy's promised bridegroom. Though I knew by now that he was quite unworthy of her, I also knew that she loved him deeply and I felt that her grief would be ten times as bitter if she learned the truth about him and how he had died. And if it came to a trial, I was afraid she might become involved in the notoriety. I wanted above all to cause her as little suffering as might be. That is my excuse for what I did next."

Rosalba thought that having killed Carlow probably disturbed Mr. Sturdy less than his own subsequent actions.

"I hid the body in a locked closet at the end of the hall and spent the night wondering what to do for the best. Towards morning I formed a plan. Chivers's death must be made to seem an accident, something that carried no overtones of scandal or disgrace. I could think of only one kind of accident which I could simulate and which would account for the injuries. If the body was found in the river, it would be assumed that the young man had fallen in, striking his head on the stony bottom, so that he drowned without regaining consciousness. By now the sun was up and I knew I must wait till the following night to put my plan into effect. Somehow I lived through the day—organizing a search for Chivers, comforting poor Dolly and her mother, feeling I was the vilest deceiver that ever lived...."

He must have been feeling even worse than I did, Rosalba realized.

"On Saturday night, after the servants had gone to bed, I somehow dragged the body down the garden and through the little gate at the end onto the riverbank. There was a good deal of light from the moon, but I could not have managed in total darkness. I was nearly exhausted and was recovering my breath when I was terrified by the sound of someone moving about a little way upstream, and I realized that there was a man fishing just below the bridge. I could not plunge my burden into the water without being seen. I waited in the shadow of the ferryman's cottage, hoping the fisherman would go away, but the trout were rising and he stayed on and on. Soon there would be others abroad, up and down the river's edge. I should have to wait for another occasion, yet I knew I had not the strength to drag the body back up the garden. I hid it in the ferryman's cottage."

"Which had already been searched on Saturday afternoon," commented Hugh.

"Yes. I could only hope that no one would trouble to look in there again, but I was very nervous, and yesterday on my return from Ashwin I was going to make sure that all was well—imagine my consternation on finding that the body had been discovered, and by you, my dear madam, a delicately nurtured lady! Though if I had known the peculiar cir-

179

cumstances—your relationship to the deceased—my horror would have been even greater."

He sounded so abject that Rosalba said, "The shock was very sudden, but you must not think I had any reason to feel affection for Carlow. He married me to suit his convenience and abandoned me without a penny, and I expect he would have done the same for Dorothy Lumm if it suited him. You saved her from a dreadful fate."

"If that is so, I am glad," said Mr. Sturdy somberly. An ingrained honesty forced him to add, "I did not strike that villain dead in order to preserve poor Dolly from a life of misery. I killed him because he was going to hold me up to public ridicule. Oh, what a vainglorious old fool I have been— unworthy to hold a position of trust!"

He burst into tears.

Hugh went to him at once. "You are too scrupulous, sir. I doubt if anyone will blame you for Carlow's death, and as for what has happened since, it must be recognized that your chief thought was for the Lumms. We can hope that the coroner's jury will bring in a verdict of death by misadventure."

Unconsoled, Mr. Sturdy continued to blubber. Rosalba felt she ought not to be witnessing his private despair. She shifted her gaze.

Hugh said to her in a low voice, "Would you wait in the next room?"

She left the two men together and went into the next room, but did not stay there. As she moved she felt something hard and heavy bang against her leg under the skirt, and remembered that she was carrying a considerable sum of money.

She left Mr. Sturdy's house, walked down the street to the Sun in Splendor, and boarded a stagecoach that was changing horses there on its way to London.

12

The unwieldy coach lumbered on through a Midland landscape which hardly seemed to alter. Rosalba had no idea what
the time was, which county they were in, nor how many
nights they would spend on the journey. This was the slowest
kind of coach, which stopped at every small town, changing
horses at every stage and often passengers as well, for many
were only traveling a short distance. Rosalba had not made
the effort to get out at any of these stops, either to stretch
her legs or take a cooling drink. She would have to, she
supposed, when they stopped for the night, and then there
would be an awkwardness at the inn because she had no
baggage with her. This was just one of the tiresome circumstances in the near future which she could not take seriously.

A very minor circumstance compared to the compelling
one of how she was going to live when her money was gone.
She had decided to go straight to Islington and try to get a
room in or near the house where her baby was being cared
for. At least she would be with Anne, the one person in the
world she had a right to love, and as soon as the little girl
was weaned they would be always together. How this was to
be managed she had no idea. Perhaps she could go back to
painting flowers and fruit on plates for the Chinaman.

Her head was aching. She closed her eyes and had a vivid
interior vision of Hugh's face, dark, intelligent and proud,
with that challenging look he used to give her just when he
was going to smile. She hadn't seen that look or the smile
lately...and now she understood why.

She had realized by now that his actions this morning had
not been quite as outrageous or as heartless as they had
seemed at the time, for she was sure that he must have suspected Mr. Sturdy and hoped that he could be induced to
confess. And of course his plan had succeeded. But that did
not excuse his cold-blooded indifference towards herself. He
would never have treated me like that, she thought, in the

old days in London when he loved me. I won't think about him anymore, she decided resolutely.

The coach was very hot, the sun beating on the windows, which had to be kept shut because of the dust. There were only two other passengers at present; a timid man who sat clasping a strongbox, as though he thought either of his companions might try to wrest it from him, and a middle-aged woman who had been scrutinizing Rosalba, and trying to talk to her, ever since joining the coach at the last stage. Rosalba parried her advances by simply ignoring questions which she considered an impertinence.

She was hardly aware how inappropriate she looked, huddled in her corner of the shabby public conveyance. Her expensive mourning was of a quality not usually worn by women who were obliged to travel unattended on a stagecoach, and the clothes themselves not really suitable for a long journey. Her flimsy muslin apron was the sort of charming frivolity ladies wore when making or receiving calls, the garlands of whitework flowers and leaves floating delicately over the somber stuff of her dress. This incongruity, combined with her youth, her beauty, her air of fatigue and deep unhappiness, was enough to stimulate curiosity.

Because the coach was so top-heavy and slow, it was continually being forced to the side of the road by other carriages, where it lurched in and out of ruts and potholes, so that the passengers were thrown about pell-mell and hard put to it not to land in each other's laps.

"Disgraceful!" exclaimed the man with the strongbox, as a post chaise flew past in a whirlwind of dust. "Those breakneck fellows ought not to be allowed on the highway."

They were approaching a village where they had to change horses yet again, and as they drew up at an inn called the Wheatsheaf it was seen that the post chaise had also stopped.

"There is a gentleman getting out and coming towards us," remarked the inquisitive woman. "I wonder what he wants."

"Let us hope he is going to apologize."

Rosalba heard this exchange but did not trouble to look through the door, which had now been opened by an inn servant asking if they wanted any refreshment.

She heard a well-known voice saying, "I have caught up with you at last, my love, and I have been able to engage a chaise, as you see, which will make our journey much more expeditious."

She gazed at Hugh in consternation. Apart from anything else he seemed to be talking complete nonsense. She heard him telling her companions that his wife had received alarming news from London and since both their local post chaises were out on hire, she had insisted on starting the journey by coach.

"And now, my dear, if you will get out, we can be on our way."

"I am not going to get out," said Rosalba, in a cool, firm voice. "Please leave me alone. And there is no need to pretend that I am your wife, when you know it is not true."

She felt a certain pleasure in giving him this metaphorical slap in the face.

"Why, I believe it is an abduction!" exclaimed the inquisitive woman. "Is this gentleman not related to you, madam?"

"No, he is not," said Rosalba, rather faintly and not daring to meet Hugh's eyes.

"Sir, you are a villain!"

"And what are you proposing to do about it?" he retorted.

The inquisitive woman did not know. She turned to the timid man, who was clasping his strongbox more tightly than ever.

"Can you not get rid of this impudent person?"

The timid man gave a squeak of protest. "It's nothing to do with me!"

"Well, I'm not so faint-hearted. Here, you!" to one of the ostlers. "Fetch the landlord!"

"Before you embark on a crusade, madam," said Hugh, "perhaps you would like to ask your protégée why she is traveling about the country without any baggage."

This was a severe shock to Rosalba's champion. She was the sort of woman who would always take the part of another woman against a man—but only so long as that other woman could claim the protection due to impregnable virtue. A much too pretty and expensively dressed young female, traveling without the smallest valise or portmanteau, was someone she could not approve; probably a runaway wife or (worse still in a different way) a runaway mistress.

The innkeeper had now arrived, as well as several more spectators; Rosalba could sense they were all on Hugh's side. He had one hand in his pocket and was carelessly jingling some loose coins. The coachman too was beginning to look askance at his unconventional passenger. Rosalba guessed that he was going to invent some excuse for getting her out of his coach.

She admitted defeat and stepped down into the yard with what dignity she could manage. She had been sitting still for so long that she found she could hardly stand and had to lean on Hugh's arm for support. It was the last straw.

They were shown into a private parlor at the back of the inn, and Hugh gave an order for tea and bread and butter.

"So you were running away from me again," he said when they were alone. "Why must you make everything so difficult, Rosalba?"

"I was trying to make our separation easier, by leaving at once without any of the awkward preliminaries."

"I suppose you decided to go after my performance this morning. I certainly behaved abominably, but surely you have known me long enough to guess that I had some purpose in view? I would have explained, if only you had waited to hear me. I was trying to force a confession out of Sturdy. I was practically certain that he was responsible for Carlow's death, and I was right."

Rosalba had guessed this much already, but she said obstinately, "I don't see how you could have known."

A waiter came in with a tray, which he set down on the table. Seeing that Rosalba made no move to pour out the tea, Hugh did so himself. It was rather weak (innkeepers being mean over such luxuries) but it smelled pleasantly aromatic. He added a drop of cream and stirred in some sugar, which Rosalba did not like.

"It will do you good," he said, handing her the tea bowl in its deep saucer.

The first sip revived her a little. She sat down and took off her hat. If Hugh was determined to justify himself, she was too exhausted to stop him.

"I suspected Sturdy," he began, "because I could see no other way of accounting for his extraordinary behavior. All the time the so-called Chivers was staying in Trilbourne, and after he disappeared, Sturdy spoke of him in the highest terms. The moment the unfortunate man's body was found in the ferryman's cottage, he became a scoundrel embroiled with Dan Robinson in some unspecified crime. Nothing was too bad for him. Yet what had happened to change the old man's opinion? You were there; you saw nothing that gave away his true character. Sturdy had no time to search the body, and Roberts, who did so, found nothing of any importance."

Rosalba reached for the teapot. "According to Sturdy, he already knew some disgraceful secret about Carlow—Chivers—which he had promised not to repeat. Surely that explained his silence."

"It didn't explain why he had not tried to prevent Dorothy from marrying a man he knew to be a villain."

"That's true. It hadn't struck me before. And he is very fond of Dorothy and her mother, isn't he?"

"Any man who can call that strapping young woman 'little Dolly' must be under some kind of spell," said Hugh, not altogether kindly. "So why had he remained passive and approving? Why hadn't he warned Dorothy against rushing into this hasty marriage with a man she hardly knew? Or persuaded Mrs. Lumm to exert her influence, written to the family lawyers in Birmingham to put them on their guard? Even if the women had refused to listen to him, he might still have achieved the necessary result. Fortune-hunters with dubious reputations can often be frightened away by the fear of being investigated; Sturdy knew that. And he could have taken all these steps without betraying the mysterious person who was supposed to have confided in him, for they were the kind of precautions that might have been taken earlier— would have been taken, I imagine, if Sturdy had been able to believe ill of a man who was willing to let him prose away about Shakespeare. So there you have it: if he knew something to the bridegroom's detriment, why had he done nothing to stop the wedding?"

185

Rosalba put down her tea bowl. She had not touched the bread and butter.

"It's a very good point, but surely it was not enough to convince you of his guilt?"

"One idea led to another. Was it possible that Sturdy had learned of Carlow's villainy only at the moment when he ceased to be a danger to Dorothy? That is to say, at the time of his death? That would explain the contradictions. Then there was the question of how and why the body had been transported to the ferryman's cottage. There was no doubt that Sturdy's house or garden was the safest and closest place from which it might have been brought. As to why it was in the cottage, clearly the dead man was eventually to be found in the river, the victim of an accident. And Sturdy had prophesied some accident all along. It was your premature discovery of the corpse, and those unaccountable injuries, which produced the curious tale of a criminal conspiracy. That convinced me."

"Did you not suspect Meade or Dan Robinson? After I told you that it was Carlow who had been killed?"

"It seemed to me that Carlow with his doting heiress was worth more alive than dead to Master Robinson. As for Meade, he could have done the killing on Friday, but he left Trilbourne before the body was moved into the ferryman's cottage."

"Good heavens, how stupid of me not to realize." Rosalba made a discovery. "I don't think I could have managed that part of the business. If I'd killed him, I mean."

"Of course you could not, my dear. That was why I had to cut such a contemptible figure this morning, when I'm afraid I used you to bait a trap."

"I don't understand."

Hugh was sitting opposite her with his elbows on the table. She noticed for the first time how drawn and strained he was.

"I suppose you do realize," he said, "what it was that broke Sturdy? The fear that he might have to commit you to prison for several months, to await trial at the next Assizes. The chances of anyone's actually hanging for the murder of Carlow were very slight—there could not be sufficient evidence—and I'm sure he calculated on that. To send Robinson for trial must have seemed to him a perfectly reasonable punishment for his share in the fraud. And if any other man, including myself, had unluckily been caught in the web— well, I think Sturdy would have kept quiet and solaced his conscience with the platitude that no innocent person is ever convicted under English law. But a woman was different. To send a young woman of breeding and sensibility into such horrors, that was something he simply would not be able to face. Or so I judged."

"You might have told me what you meant to do."

"There was no time. I had to act at once, before Dan Robinson was caught and gave away the fact that the dead man was your first husband. If Sturdy heard that from a third party, if he'd had time to think logically before he questioned you, he was bound to realize that the case against you was not so very strong after all. If I wanted to wring a confession out of him, I had to take you to his house immediately, so that the shock of the disclosure should come to him while you were there in the room, vulnerable and apparently defenseless. I made everything sound as black as possible. He lost his head. I thought he would."

"I think that was very cruel. To us both. As though we were just two pieces in a monstrous game of chess."

He flinched a little. Then he said, "Shall I tell you what would have happened if Sturdy hadn't confessed? Carlow's name would have come out at the inquest—I am afraid that is inevitable, by the way. His death would have remained a mystery. Rumor and conjecture would have spread among people who had no real grasp of the evidence, and for the rest of our lives you and I would have been suspected of conspiring together to murder your first husband. Rather a grim future, don't you agree? I hope you will forgive me for using such brutal means to avert it."

She was a good deal shaken. "I hadn't considered—it would have been horrible. But how quickly your mind must have worked."

"Danger is a sharp spur. Now that I have explained my infamous behavior, I hope you'll change your mind about leaving me."

"That wasn't why I left you."

187

He studied her anxiously. "Why, then?"

"Since our marriage was invalid, we may as well admit it was a mistake. You could not trust me—"

"And you could not trust me either. We made a bad start, but can we not allow each other a second chance?"

"You can hardly wonder at my distrusting your machinations this morning—"

"Never mind this morning. I am speaking of the past fortnight. I know you didn't deceive me deliberately—I was wrong there and I'm very sorry for it. But when you found out that Carlow was alive, why couldn't you turn to me, instead of sending for that damned attorney?"

She was taken off her guard, not knowing how to answer. You were so distant and unkind...I thought you were disappointed in me...I thought you might be wishing you could marry Alicia..."

In the end she blurted out the real reason, the one that had counted most, even while she had felt so forlorn and unwanted in Trilbourne.

"I was afraid you'd send me away. Back to Hunsden Street."

"To Hunsden Street? Why should I?" He sounded astonished.

"Well, you wouldn't have let me stay in your aunt's house when it turned out that we weren't properly married. Would you?" she added doubtfully, seeing his baffled expression.

"My dear girl, that's exactly what I was doing! You forget, I knew much sooner than you did that we weren't properly married. It was one of the circumstances that was making me so bad-tempered. I was angry and wretched, but you'll notice I couldn't bring myself to take any step which might have led even to a temporary separation."

He got up and came round the table.

"Are you going to give me that second chance, my little white rose?"

"I wish you would not call me that, it sounds so absurd."

"Is that why you are crying?"

"I'm not crying. Not very much," said Rosalba as she cast herself into his arms. "Hugh, why must you always win every argument?"

"It is a very disobliging habit," he said humbly, between kisses.

The kisses went on for some time, becoming less anguished and more enjoyable. Then they had to call a halt and decide what must be done next. Could she face the drive back to Trilbourne this evening? The journey which had taken so long in the bumbling old coach would be over in a couple of hours, if they were traveling post.

"But I can't go back," she said in a panic. "Your family must know about Carlow by now, and that I am just your mistress."

"They want you to go back, to remain under their roof until I can get the legal formalities cleared up and arrange our second wedding. My aunt informed me that she honors you for your praiseworthy delicacy of mind."

"For my *what?*"

Hugh smiled. "When you ran away, they thought you had only found out yesterday that Carlow was still alive at the time of our marriage. They thought that was your sole reason for leaving, and I'm afraid I didn't enlighten them. They have all become very much attached to you," he added more seriously. "They are determined to stand by us and ignore any ripples of scandal there may be."

Rosalba was touched. She did not see how anyone could have become fond of the dismal, brooding creature she had been for the last few weeks. But the Rainhams had always been kind, all of them except Olivia, and perhaps she would always have been jealous of anyone her brother married.

Hugh and Rosalba decided to dine before they set out. They could never remember afterwards what they had to eat, only that she had absently poured custard over a slice of roast pork.

Bowling northwards in a well-sprung carriage, she lay back against Hugh's shoulder with his arm round her, in a state of blissful serenity. Too tired for passion (that would return soon enough), they were wonderfully united and at peace. They did not talk much, but there were still some things she was curious to know.

"How did you answer Henry Carlow's letter?"

"I'm ashamed to say I never answered it at all. However, I shall have to do so now."

"I hope you will not be obliged to lay any blame on John Meade. Which reminds me, why do you suppose he left Trilbourne on Saturday morning? Had he given up the hunt for Carlow?"

"A maidservant at Carlow's lodging has only just remembered that there was a strange gentleman asking for him on the Friday evening, after he left the house. I presume that was Meade. If so, he would have heard all the talk next day about the disappearance of Edward Chivers. He probably concluded that the news of an inquiring stranger had been enough to make Carlow take to his heels."

A little later she asked, "What will happen to poor Mr. Sturdy?"

"He will have to resign from the magistracy. Nothing worse, I hope. I don't think anyone will believe he meant to kill Carlow, for most people will consider his motive far too slight. Unlike ours."

"It does sound trivial: to kill a man because he threatens to make you look a fool."

"Oh, I don't think that was his reason," said Hugh calmly. "Sturdy struck out at the man who had first created and then destroyed the most precious illusion he had ever entertained—the dream of having discovered an unknown play by Shakespeare. There may have been murder in his heart, but no one else need ever know it."

Rosalba slept a little. When she came to life again, Hugh was cradling her in his arms. She sat up and rubbed her eyes.

"Why didn't you wake me? You must have the most shocking cramp."

"You looked so young. I think we must bring Anne up here as soon as we can. Perhaps when we move from Bridge Place."

"Are we going to Ashwin with Alicia?" Rosalba took care to sound cheerful and acquiescent.

"Good God, no. Alicia is a dear girl, I would do anything to help her, but to live in her climate of perpetual nervous anxiety is more than I could stand. She makes me feel as though I ought to be walking on tiptoe."

Rosalba was rather glad to hear this.

They were driving through a lovely valley full of the scents of summer; the countryside seemed to breathe audibly after the heat of the day, the trees were darkening in silhouette against a pale, luminous sky. Hugh was talking about a place where they might settle: used sometimes as a dower house, and now standing empty after the departure of a tenant who had leased it for several years, it was about three miles from Trilbourne in a village she had not yet visited.

Hugh hoped she would be comfortable there but sounded slightly apprehensive. She wondered what was wrong with the house. Old and poky, perhaps, with damp kitchens and a north-facing aspect into the side of a hill. She made cautious inquiries.

But Knighton, it seemed, was only fifty years old, with well-proportioned rooms, sash windows, a fine staircase and every convenience from spacious attics down to a well-lit basement. There was a little Doric temple in the garden, and by rooting out an old hedge they would be able to open up a wide prospect of river and woodland.... It might be interesting to make such improvements.

By now she understood his slight hesitation. He thought she might be dull in such a quiet place. Eventually they would be able to spend more time in London, he assured her, and make their promised Continental tour. He had never thought of her as a countrywoman.

Yet she had been quite content in the country with her mother, never aimless or dissatisfied. To become the mistress of a house like Knighton would always have fulfilled her greatest ambition—provided she was married to the right man. That was the crucial test. Loneliness might be more endurable in the crowded variety of a town. Companionship would be deeper and more perfect in the country.

She turned to Hugh, her eyes shining.

"I'm sure I shall be happy at Knighton," she said, with a conviction she had not felt since she was a child.